Into the Sunset

S.L. STERLING

Into the Sunset

Copyright © 2022 by S.L. Sterling

All rights reserved. Without limiting the rights under copyright reserved about, no part of this publication may be reproduced, stored in, or introduced into a retrieval system, or transmitted in any form or by any means (mechanical, electronic, photocopying, recording, or otherwise) without the prior written permission of both the copyright owner and the above publisher of the book. This is a work of fiction. Any references to historical events, real people, or real places are used fictitiously. Other names, characters, places, and events are products of the author's imagination, and any resemblance to actual events or places or persons, living or dead, is entirely coincidental. Disclaimer: This book contains mature content not suitable for those under the age of 18. It involves strong language and sexual situations. All parties portrayed in sexual situations are consenting adults over the age of 18.

ISBN: 978-1-989566-19-0

Paperback ISBN: 978-1-989566-31-2

Editor: Brandi Aquino, Editing Done Write

Cover Design: Thunderstruck Cover Design

Chapter One

Ben - June 2015

I pulled into Jessica's driveway and checked my pocket for the twentieth time since I left the house, feeling the outline of the item it held. I swallowed hard and turned up the music, trying to calm my nerves. We both graduated from college yesterday, and we were setting out to celebrate together. I was about to get out of the car and go to the door when the porch light turned on.

The inside door opened, and Jessica came walking down the front steps. She looked amazing, her long blonde hair flowing freely behind her, tight jeans that hugged her in all the right places, and a white T-shirt with a matching jean jacket over top. I watched as she bounced down the stairs and smiled as she waved excitedly at me. Seconds later, she pulled the door open and hopped in, my car filling with the light scent of the jasmine perfume I had gotten her for her birthday a few weeks earlier.

"Hey," I said, leaning over and meeting her lips. "You ready to go?"

"MMMM... yes." She hummed as she kissed my lips. "Exactly what did you have in mind for tonight? Where are we going?" she asked, kissing me one more time before pulling her seatbelt across her.

"Let's go find out, shall we." I winked and reversed out of the driveway.

We drove up the coast, Jessica looking out over the water at the sailboats that were making their way into the harbor. It was a sight I would never tire of. I loved our small town and looked forward to settling down with Jessica by my side. I reached over and took her hand in mine as I turned down an old dirt road and continued driving until we came to a crossroads. I made a left and pulled the car into a makeshift driveway.

"I thought we would come out here, to the site my dad and I have been working on. This way we can have some privacy, and I can show you what we've done to this old place."

"You guys are working on this? I've always loved this place. From the time I was a little girl I always wondered who used to live here, what they were like." She undid her seatbelt and slowly climbed out of the car into a field of overgrown grass. She smiled as she shut the door and looked in the direction of the old house.

We'd come out here last summer, and she had talked about what it would be like to fix up this old place together. She meandered toward the house, smiling to herself.

Reaching into the backseat of my car, I pulled out the red-checkered blanket and the picnic basket that I'd packed earlier and caught up to her. She was already up near the frame of the recent addition that we'd added. She looked around, a slight smile on her face.

"You're adding on to it?"

"Yes, it was rather small, so my dad decided it would help sell if it was larger. It's only a frame now, but once the walls go up, it will be so much easier to envision," I said, dropping the blanket and basket down in a grassy area that had been recently cut.

I walked over and began showing her where things

would go. "I know it doesn't look like much now, but just wait."

"I'm sure it will be amazing. It's a shame though. I always loved this old house the way it was, but I can't wait to see what it looks like once it's finished."

She had looked around a little more, and I took the opportunity to spread the blanket out on the ground. Then I walked over to where she was standing and grabbed her hand. "Come with me," I said, slightly pulling her in the direction of the blanket. "I brought us a picnic."

"That sounds wonderful. What are we having?"

I waited for Jessica to sit down first, then she patted the space next to her, looking up at me with her blue eyes. I knelt down, removing the small light from the picnic basket, and turned it on, lighting up the area in which we sat. I pulled out our dinner and opened the lids on the containers. "I hope you're hungry and that roast chicken and potato salad are okay?" I questioned.

"That sounds wonderful. I'm so hungry. It was so busy at work today that I didn't really have time to eat."

I reached into the basket and pulled out two forks, handing one to her. Then as we always had done, we took turns digging into each dish. We ate, talking about graduation and our plans for the future, as the crickets started their evening song. Once we had finished dinner and we put the containers back in the car, I rolled my jacket up under my head and lay back, staring up at the stars, Jessica cuddling into my side.

"One day, I want us to build us a house like this," I whispered, kissing her forehead. "Our master bedroom will have a skylight so we can fall asleep looking up at the stars like we've done since we were kids. I will give you your dream country kitchen that you've been telling me you want. We'll have a second bedroom for when our little ones come along, and in the backyard, I'll build them a tree house, like the one I had in my backyard growing up," I whispered.

"You mean like the one I fell out of when I was ten and broke my arm." Jess laughed into my neck.

"If that is how you remember it, yes." I laughed, squeezing her side playfully. "It was also one that you would sneak into on a weekly basis to fool around with me after our parents thought we were fast asleep. The same one Jules caught us in," I said, kissing her.

A cool wind blew over us, and Jess snuggled her nose into my neck and kissed me lightly on the cheek. "I'd love that. It will be like our dreams come true."

I wrestled with giving her what was in my pocket, until my stomach turned rapidly, threatening to redeem its contents. I had saved almost every penny I made working for my father over the last four years for the ring, and I prayed that she liked it. She hummed lightly in my ear while she rested her head on my shoulder, and that was when I decided I needed to take a chance and do it.

I reached my hand into my pocket and felt the ring that had been waiting there for me. I pulled it from my pocket and pushed myself up on my elbow, carefully holding her.

"What are you doing?" she asked, looking up at me.

"I know it's not much, but it's what I could afford right now," I said, holding the ring out for her.

Her fingertips grazed mine as she took the ring from me. "It's beautiful."

"I want to marry you, Jess. I want us to start our lives together."

I dropped the ring into her hand, and she slipped it onto her finger, then held her hand out to look at it.

"It's just a promise ring." I swallowed.

"It's perfect."

"It's perfect for now, but, one day, when I can afford it, I will get you a genuine diamond ring. That's just your birthstone."

"It's perfect, Ben. I love it, and I love you."

I leaned down and kissed her deeply, then I lay back once again, pulling her against me, and we looked up at the night sky.

Chapter Two

I glanced down at my watch as I ran through the mall. Of course I was late. I was always late. I rounded the corner and spotted Alison immediately as I made my way into the mall's food court. She sat there sipping on a pop, grinning, and waving like a lunatic as I approached her. I couldn't help but laugh.

"Hey, girl, it's about time you got here," she said, standing to give me an enormous hug.

"Yeah, sorry, I got out of work late, and then the bus was late," I explained, sliding into the seat across from her and stealing a sip of her drink.

"Why did you take the bus? Where is Ben? I

figured he would drive you," Alison said, looking over my shoulder in the direction I'd come.

"He would have, but his father told him he needed to stay and work tonight. They are working on that old house on the edge of town, you know that one I love." I sighed. "I feel like I barely see him anymore now that he's been working full time." I glanced once again at my cell phone to see if he had messaged me, and then popped my phone into my purse when Alison squealed out loud.

"What on earth is that on your finger? Let me see! Let me see!" she said, reaching across the table and grabbing my hand.

I let out a breath and held out my hand that sported the promise ring Ben had given me three months ago. It was the first time I had worn it outside of when I had seen Ben. The only reason I had worn it today was because I was supposed to meet Ben for lunch and had forgotten to take it off before I came here. At first, it was fear of losing it, but as more time had passed on, something much deeper inside of me kept me from wearing it, something I couldn't put my finger on.

"I can't believe I didn't know about this. How have you kept it a secret for so long? My God, you are so lucky. Ben is such a sweetheart, not to mention hot!" Alison fanned herself as I giggled.

"Thanks," I said, pulling my hand away and hiding it under the table.

"What's wrong?

"Nothing, why?" I swallowed hard.

"Jess, I would have thought you'd be excited. He wants you, and he has a great future ahead of him, unlike some other guys around here," Alison said, looking at me as if I were crazy for feeling the way I was. Out of all the guys in our town, I had lucked out and gotten one of the excellent ones.

"It's just...I don't know," I said, letting out a breath. "I'm bored, I guess. I looked at my parents the other day, both of them raised here, both of them will die here. They've never experienced the world. I don't want the same. I want out of this sleepy, tiny town. I want to explore the world, and all Ben wants is to keep us here. I brought up moving the other day, wanting to settle somewhere else, and we got into the biggest fight we've ever had." I sighed.

"Well, I am sure you guys can come to a compromise. Can't you?"

"I wish it were that way, but when I spoke to him about it last night, he was adamant that this was the way things would have to be. He wants to work with his father, which is great, and I understand that, but it's almost as if he has our entire lives planned out already. I know he will take over his father's business one day, but that doesn't mean he can't do it from another town. Plus, I feel as if I barely see him. He is always working, and when he comes home, he is so exhausted he doesn't want to do anything. He also wants to build us a house, he even has the interior planned out, and he keeps talking about having kids. I mean, he literally has it all planned. He's never really even asked me what I wanted."

"Girl, give it time. I'm sure he doesn't have everything planned out."

I smiled. "No, he does, right down to our kids' names. Anyways, are we ready to shop?" I said, getting up and stretching. This was not a subject I wanted to talk about tonight. I just wanted to forget all about it and carry on like we used to, before all the pressure.

"Jess..." Alison said, grabbing my hand.

"No, let's go, come on. I don't want to talk about it anymore," I said, pulling away and heading toward one of our favorite stores.

An hour later, we had almost covered the entire mall without mention of Ben or the situation and were now heading into the last area of the mall. Carrying our bags, we rounded the corner, and that was where I saw it. I had remembered seeing an advertisement for the Great Model Search coming to our area a few months ago, and I pulled on Alison's arm to get her attention.

"What is this?" Alison questioned, coming up beside me and glancing at one flyer that hung on the wall. "Oh wait, I heard about this. It's that model search thing. You can win a modeling contract if they choose you."

"Yes, they advertised it a while back, and I totally forgot they were coming here. Basically, they ask you some questions, take a few pictures of you, and if someone sees your mini portfolio and likes you, you could get a contract," I said approaching the booth and ringing the bell that sat on the counter.

"What are you doing?" Alison asked, gripping my hand as the bell rang out.

"I'm going to give it a shot, just for fun."

"Seriously, Jessica, come on. Let's go. Not only will your parents kill you, but it will piss Ben off."

"Relax. I just want to get some information, that's it. They won't be calling me. I mean, look at me," I said, throwing my arms out to my sides. "I'm a mess."

Alison let out a laugh at my gesture. "You, my friend, are not a mess." She giggled, and then we heard a lady's voice ask, "Can I help you, ladies."

"Oh, hi! I am interested in--" I hadn't even gotten the words out of my mouth when she shoved a clipboard and pen into my hand.

"Fill these forms out, and as soon as you return the release forms and the attached questionnaire, we will take a couple quick photos." She turned and walked away before I could ask her questions.

I looked at Alison and shrugged, then looked down at the forms, then back to Alison, and walked over and took a seat on a bench. She sat down beside me and pulled out her phone while I began filling out the three forms. A half hour later, I was in a changing room with some select outfits. I changed into the first one and stepped out behind the camera where the impatient lady took a bunch of photos. Then she directed me to change into the next outfit. This went on until I had been photographed in all of the outfits in every position possible.

"Are you sure your friend isn't interested?" the lady asked through the curtain as I finished changing back into my own clothes.

"Yeah, I'm sure," I mumbled.

"It's an exceptional opportunity. She should give it a go."

I let out a laugh. "She won't. This isn't her kind of thing, so don't bother."

"That's too bad. Okay, well, that is all." She dismissed me, pulling the card out of the camera.

"Thanks," I muttered.

Once I changed, I grabbed my purse and looked over at the bench where Alison sat looking at her phone. She looked bored out of her mind. I felt bad for making her wait so long and was hoping she wasn't too angry with me.

"Have you traveled the world enough now?" she asked, annoyed, as she looked at her watch when I approached her. "Ben called me looking for you, since you didn't answer your phone. He didn't sound very happy."

"You didn't tell him what I was doing, did you?" I questioned as I grabbed my bags from beside her.

"No, I just said you were in a change room trying on clothes and that I had your purse."

"Great, thanks. I'm sorry about making you wait. It was so fun, and for a minute, I caught a glimpse of what it would be like to be in that world, but it was probably a waste of time because they sure won't be calling me. Let's go." I pulled my phone from my purse and quickly sent a text to Ben.

Chapter Three

BEN - FEBRUARY 2016

It was Friday night, and Jess and I sat in my car in silence, looking out over the view of the city. This was another one of our special quiet places to come and be together and watch the twinkling lights from the city below.

"It's beautiful up here," Jessica murmured.

A breeze blew, and I caught the scent of the cherry blossoms in the air. "So what made you want to come all the way up here?" I asked, taking hold of Jessica's hand and bringing it to my lips. "We could have gone to the drive-in or something," I whispered against the skin of her hand. I knew she was unhappy at her job and had been looking for another one for a while. I'd even gone so far as to ask my father if there was anything he could provide her with, but he said he had no openings at the time.

"I wanted to talk to you about something." Jess smiled and looked over at me.

I felt the unease in her stare, and suddenly I was afraid of what she had to say. I knew Jess had been struggling with other things since we had graduated college, but other than the job issues, she wouldn't tell me with what. I sensed it was a change with all our friends; our social circle had gotten smaller since graduating as most of our friends had moved away.

"Six months ago, they held a model search at the mall. I had totally forgotten they were even coming. Anyway, I filled out their application form and had some pictures taken."

"What would you do that for?"

Jessica shrugged and reached down into her bag and pulled a brown envelope from her purse and handed it to me.

"What is this?" I questioned.

"Open it!" she said, clasping her hands together and bringing them up under her chin like she did whenever she was excited about something.

I could read the excitement in her eyes, and so I opened the envelope and pulled out a thick stack of papers. On top sat some beautiful images of Jessica, which I flipped through slowly, taking them in. "These are amazing pictures of you. It was nice of them to send them to you. I love this one," I said, holding up what I thought was one of the best shots of her.

"Yeah, they are great, but that isn't all they sent me," she said, the excitement building in her voice again. She reached over and pulled the images off the thick pile of paperwork, producing a contract. "Two weeks ago, they called and presented me with an enormous opportunity, and here it is! All in black and white." She squealed. "It almost killed me to wait to tell you, but I wanted to have the contract in hand before I said anything."

I began reading the letter that sat on top. Words like contract, Los Angeles, Las Vegas, moving. They were the ones that jumped out at me, and I felt my chest getting tight at the mere idea of her going away. I swallowed hard. "What does all this mean, Jessica?"

"It means they are offering me a modeling contract, Ben. It's my dream come true. I'll get to model and see the sights, and I am so excited that I wanted to share this with you in our special place."

I swallowed hard. "What did your parents say?" I asked as I sat there trying to focus and re-read the letter, but it did little good, so I started flipping through the bundle of paperwork.

"They were angry. Furious, actually," she said, picking at one of her nails.

"Are... Are you going to go?" I asked. I could feel tightness in my chest that hadn't been there before, but now that I'd asked her the question, it didn't seem to want to let up. I didn't want to see her happiness disappear, but at the same time I was terrified of her answer.

"Well, I thought that perhaps you would want to go with me. I'm sure my parents would feel better about it if you did. Plus, there is so much opportunity out there, and it would only be for a little while. I mean, the contract is only for a year. I want you to go with me."

My stomach hurt at the thought of her leaving me, and it was getting harder and harder for me to breathe. It reminded me of the time that I had gotten tackled in one of my high school football games. The guy had come charging at me and knocked me flat on my ass. I hadn't even seen him coming. When we collided, I went flying, and when I landed, he had knocked the air right out of me. This was no different. She had tackled me, just differently.

"Jess, I don't think I can. I mean, our business is here. My father needs me."

"Sure you can, come on. You can build and remodel homes anywhere. You can do exactly what you're doing now."

"Unfortunately, I can't. Dad's company is here. We have worked hard to make Sunset Builders what they are today. I can't just leave him. Especially not after my mom walked out on him. He needs Julie and I. Besides, we are working on numerous renovations, some that I am in charge of."

"Well, it's only for a little while. What about if I go and we try a long-distance relationship?"

"Nothing about a year is short. It's a long time, Jess. I want to build my life with you in it, not build it with you being halfway across the country. Besides, what if you decide you like it so much out there that you don't want to return?"

"Then come with me."

I closed my eyes and leaned my head back against the headrest. I could barely catch my breath. My heart was beating so hard it was making me dizzy. It hurt to breathe, and when I opened my eyes, the lights of the city were hazy and seemed so far away.

"Ben, please. This is so important to me. I need this."

I sat quietly for a few minutes, not saying anything, then I looked over at Jess, at her beautiful pleading eyes, and shook my head. "Jess, I'm sorry. There is no way I can go. I just can't drop the projects I am working on, and I won't abandon my father."

The minute the words had left my lips, she quickly

turned away from me. She wiped a tear from her cheek, making me feel like even more of an ass. I was about to reach over and take her hand in mine, to calm her down and explain to her how I felt about this, but she spoke first.

"Why is it that everything is always about you?" she bit out, reaching over and ripping the pile of papers from my hand and shoving them back in the envelope. "Take me home."

"Jess, come on. I don't want to fight with you. Let's talk about this."

"There isn't anything more to talk about. You've made your thoughts and feelings on this subject perfectly clear. You want me to stay here and be your dutiful little homemaker. Just take me home, please."

I didn't want us to leave for the night angry at one another. She seemed adamant, and it terrified me that she wouldn't talk to me about this, to find some sort of compromise. Jess was stubborn when she got angry. I couldn't look at her, so I turned and looked out my window. I did not want to watch any more of her tears. I couldn't because they were tears I had caused.

"Please, Ben, just take me home," she whispered.

I looked over at her, but she had her head turned away from me. I let out a sigh, then started the engine and backed out of the spot we were parked.

The drive home felt like forever. Neither of us

spoke. Jessica just kept wiping her face with the back of her hand, making me feel even worse than I had before. When we pulled into her driveway, I turned to apologize and tell her I loved her and that we would figure out a way to make it work, but when I went to speak, she shoved her hand at me, her fist closed.

"What is this?" I questioned.

"It's your ring. I can't do this. It's always your way, everything. You've never even asked me what I want. You just assumed I wanted a house full of kids. I refuse to live my life this way."

My heart ripped in two when she dropped the ring into the palm of my hand. I looked down at the ring I had saved for, and before I was able to say anything, she was out of the car and running toward her front door.

My fingers closed around the ring as I watched her close the inside door. I sat there, looking at the ring, once again trying to catch my breath, trying to decide if I should try to talk to her tonight, but the porch light went off. I knew if I went to the door, her parents would wake, so I decided that I would let her cool off for the night.

Ten minutes later, I set the ring on my bedside table and flopped face down on my bed. She didn't mean what she said, I was sure of it, or maybe I was just trying to convince myself. I'd sleep on it and go over first thing in the morning to talk to her. I was sure that after a good night's sleep on both our parts, we'd talk, and everything would go back to normal.

It felt as if it had been the longest day of my life that I'd had on the job site in a long time. I'd woken up late, and just when I was going to tell my father that I'd be late, an emergency had broken out on one of the job sites and he needed me to fill in. Of course, I was irritated, and even minor things were bothering me way more than they normally did. Once my father returned from dealing with the issues, he had pulled me aside later in the afternoon because I'd had a disagreement with one worker and he'd submitted a complaint. That had just added more fuel to the already building flames inside of me.

I drove through the city, not bothering to go home first to shower. Instead, I made my way over to Jessica's house. She hadn't messaged me throughout the day, but I hoped that by the time I got to her house she would at least speak with me. I had given everything she had said a great deal of thought while I had worked throughout the day, and I realized that I hadn't really been fair. She had been right; I'd never asked her about anything, and I hoped that we could come take some time and talk, to come to an agreement, so we could move on.

As I pulled around the corner, I frowned. A police car sat in her driveway. I pulled in beside the car and cut the engine, then hopped out and ran up to the front door. While I waited for it to be opened, I felt my breast pocket, feeling the outline of the ring. I wanted my girl to have what she deserved. I wanted to make sure she knew she was supported in whatever she wanted to do. I'd given us a lot of thought over the course of the day, and I was excited to tell her that if she wanted to take the modeling job then I would start looking for a job outside of the city.

With a smile on my face, I reached up and knocked hard on the front door again and waited. When the door wasn't pulled open with the usual speed, I reached up and knocked again. Finally, I heard the locks unlatch, and the door opened. Jessica's mom stood there, her cheeks tear streaked and her eyes red.

"Ben, thank God. Perhaps you can help us," she said, pushing the door open and signaling for me to step inside.

"What's wrong?" I questioned, that familiar burn in my chest coming back.

"We didn't know what to do, so we called the police. Jessica's gone. All she left was this note." She leaned over and handed me the single slip of paper. I slowly read the words printed in Jessica's beautifully neat handwriting, and that was when the tears built behind my eyes. She was gone. I had driven her away. I was the only one to blame.

Chapter Four

JESSICA - FEBRUARY 2016

I woke well before the alarm went off and I lay on the lumpy mattress thinking about what I had gotten myself into. I'd been in Vegas for six months now, and I missed home something terrible. Over that time, I found that there had been little truth in the letter that had accompanied the contract that I had received. Instead of having a fully furnished flat all to myself, as promised, I was stuck sharing it with eight other girls. It was nothing special. They furnished it with half broken furniture, and we had little to no privacy, but it was free. That part had been right. The modeling aspect hadn't been what I thought it would be, either. Actually, for the most part, it was non-existent.

Right from the start, they barked orders that we all needed to lose weight, eat better, and exercise more. Most days there were people who followed us around yelling at us about our posture. During the entire first month of me being here, someone had reminded me daily that I was not perfect and they picked me and the other girls apart over and over, until we practically broke down. I'd concluded that they wanted us all to be nothing but unhealthy anorexic chicks, with little to no backbone, and that was exactly what I was becoming.

I didn't waste any time. I got up and headed for the shower before the others woke. Today was the day we were meeting with some agents, and by nine I sat in the waiting room of some agency with twenty other girls, all tired and exhausted. I had been lucky enough to sign two small deals since I had been here, nothing huge, but today was apparently the day of truth. It was the day that these agents were making their picks. It apparently would help me that I'd already signed two deals, but I was told for anything substantial, I would need an agent.

I looked around the room at all the girls sitting there. Then I laughed to myself as I wondered how I had gone from wanting this so badly to sitting here silently praying that they wouldn't call my name. In the past few months, I had realized probably more than ever that Ben had been right all along. This wasn't for me, it wasn't what I wanted, and I yearned to be back in the safety of his arms and my childhood bedroom.

I looked down at my phone, debating on whether I should text him or just surprise him when I returned. I couldn't wait to leave this meeting, get a bus ticket, and head back to that boring tiny town. I'd hoped he'd be waiting for me, but somewhere deep down inside I had a feeling he wouldn't be. I'd treated him terribly, and it would serve me right that he had moved on.

I let out a breath. The longer I sat there watching these girls get called, the greater the itch to go home became. I was one of the last people in the room, and I looked down at my watch. It was almost five. I'd spent the entire day here. I began collecting my things and was just about to the door when a man called my name. I turned and looked in his direction. He was an attractive-looking man, with steel-grey eyes that popped against his black hair.

I swallowed hard, keeping my back straight, exactly how I'd been taught. His gaze skimmed my body as I crossed the room and greeted him. There was no talk. He just stepped to the side, allowing me to pass by him and enter into his office, and then I felt his hand land on my lower back, guiding me forward.

"Take a seat," he said, closing the door behind him to give us privacy.

I did as I was told, but silently I prayed that he would tell me I wasn't good enough and just send me packing. I was tired. Tired of all the working out, makeup sessions, primping sessions, and photo shoots we had done, along with all the diet restrictions. What I really wanted was to curl up with a movie, a bottle of coke, and an entire pepperoni pizza all to myself. Instead, I sat here feeling sorry for myself that no one-- not one agent--had called upon me. I had given up.

He sat down across from me, shuffled a few papers around, and then clasped his large hands on the desk in front of him and smiled. "Jessica, I have your photos, and I have to say, u. You, my dear, have such potential. I'm honestly surprised no one has grabbed you already."

Instantly, I perked up. Apparently, no matter how bad I thought I wanted to return home, there was still a part of me that wanted so badly to believe that all of this had not been for nothing. I still wanted my break, but as I waited for him to speak, suddenly I realized I was still so torn. Part of me was secretly praying that I could just go back to my insignificant life, where no one knew me, and sleep in my bed, but there was an enormous part of me praying that my big break would come.

"I'm Kendrick Hayward." He held his large, powerful hand out for me to shake. As my hand slid into his, a shot of lightning flowed through my body, and as soon as my eyes met his, I felt a tremor in my tummy. Up close, he was a really attractive man. His features were sharp, he dressed the part, and the scent of his cologne enveloped me.

"Nice to meet you," I said, placing my hands back in my lap.

"I know many people, Jessica. I can get you deals with all the big names. It takes time, but I have a lot more pull than many of the agents you've encountered. I've been in this business for a long time, and I'd be thrilled if you would be my pet project, if you will."

I couldn't help the smile that formed on my lips. I also couldn't help the nagging feeling I felt in the pit of my stomach. Kendrick was an extremely attractive man, and the longer we talked, the longer I sat looking at him, I started having thoughts that I probably shouldn't be having about a man who was nearly double my age.

"What do you say? Let me take you from where you are right now, to a career you've probably only ever dreamed about."

"Why me?" I laughed nervously. "I mean, I know it sounds like I'm not confident in my ability, but the others are so much more experienced than me."

Kendrick stood and poured us two glasses of water, then handed me mine and walked back around and sat down behind the enormous oak desk. "Well, I see something in you that I don't see in the others. You're-- and please don't take this the wrong way, but I've been watching you. You're special," he said, winking at me.

I couldn't help but feel the excitement building in me at his words. His calm demeanor, his charming voice, instantly put me at ease. What would I tell the other girls when they asked? Would they be jealous that I got discovered and they didn't? Would they hate living with me now?

"Tell you what, I have to be at a party tonight. Why don't you come with me as my guest? There will be many people there, the right people, and this will give me the opportunity to introduce you to those people."

I sat there, dumbfounded, not knowing what to say. I was excited and could feel my insides vibrating as Kendrick sat across from me waiting for my answer. In those few minutes, I had forgotten about all the hard work it had taken to be sitting in this spot. I had forgotten about the grueling workouts, the minimal amounts of food I'd eaten over the past few months, and the roughly thirty pounds I had already lost in those short six months, when in fact I hadn't needed to lose any weight to begin with. Over the course of the next two hours that I spent with Kendrick, I'd also forgotten about Ben and my longing to return to my hometown.

"What do you say?" he asked, glancing at his watch. "I'll pick you up at eight."

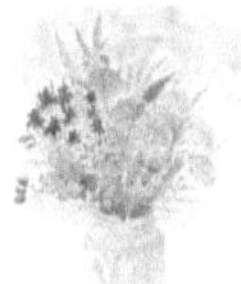

Kendrick had done exactly as promised. He had introduced me to people as we made our way through the room. The glitz and glamour blinded me as I looked at all these people. They weren't the only thing blinding me; I was also blinded by all the promises that Kendrick kept whispering in my ear as his roaming hands touched me in places they shouldn't have. He introduced me to everyone we had come into contact with.

After a while, Kendrick asked that I stand off to the side while he spoke to a group of other agents, so I complied, and now I stood off in the corner sipping on a glass of ice water, while he spoke with a group of men across the way. I watched him, talking, laughing, and drinking down glasses of scotch as if they were water.

Sipping on my water, I looked around the room and noticed an incredibly attractive woman standing beside me. At first glance, I thought I recognized her as she too sipped on a glass of water. A man came up to her and exchanged her almost-empty glass for a full one and kissed her on the cheek before he walked on over to the same group of men Kendrick was speaking with.

It was only a matter of moments before she caught me staring at her. She looked at me and smiled. "Hi, I'm Kate," she said, holding out her hand to me. "Quite the party isn't it."

"Jessica." I smiled back, shaking her hand. "Yes, it is," I said, glancing around the room.

"I've never seen you around here before. You must be new."

"I am. I just signed on with an agent today." I knew her from somewhere. I just couldn't place her.

"That's fantastic. Any big contracts on the horizon yet? I just signed on with Victoria's Secret."

As soon as she said that, I immediately knew who she was. I swallowed hard, trying not to seem too anxious. "You're Kate Green aren't you?"

"Yes." She smiled, setting her glass down on the table beside us. "So who have you signed with? Let me guess, John Nolan or Patrick Johnson?"

"Kendrick Hayward. He's right there. He said he just had to step away to discuss signing me with Calvin Klein."

I noticed Kate followed my line of sight as I nodded toward where Kendrick stood.

"I see. He's an attractive man, isn't he?"

I followed her gaze and saw she was looking in Kendrick's direction. "Yes."

"Somewhat…" I watched as she brought her finger to her lips in thought. "Impressive, at first."

"Yes, very." I smiled.

When I looked back to her, she nodded at me and somewhat smiled. "He seems to have a lot of connections, doesn't he?"

I nodded and smiled at her as she stepped a little closer to me.

"I don't want to burst your bubble because that really isn't my style, but be careful with Kendrick. He isn't what he seems."

My stomach sank at her words, and I was about to ask her what she meant by that when we were interrupted by the gentleman who had been with her earlier. "Dear, we need to get going," he whispered, putting his hand on her lower back. "Early-morning meetings tomorrow."

"Okay, love," she said, placing her hand on his back and leaning in to kiss him on the cheek. She said nothing as they stepped away, leaving me wondering what she had meant by her comment. I continued to watch as the man pulled her off into the crowd, but she stopped, signaling to him to give her just a moment. She came back through the crowd and shoved a card into my hand. "If you need anything, call."

She was gone before I could look down at the card. Simple words: Kate Green, and a phone number below her name. I shoved the card into my purse just in time for Kendrick to come over to me. I could smell the scotch on his breath as he leaned in and kissed my cheek.

"How did it go? Anything?"

"My dear, these things take time. Have patience," he slurred in my ear. "We should get going," he said, pulling me through the crowd.

Ten minutes later, I found myself in the front seat of Kendrick's car, holding on for dear life, while he raced into the city back to his apartment.

Chapter Five

BEN - OCTOBER 2016

A cool rush of fall air blew as I packed the last of my tools into the back of my truck and looked up to the finished house. The renovation had taken longer than we expected, but I was so glad that we had finally finished this old rundown house. Driving down that dirt road every day was like driving a screwdriver into my chest. It held one too many bittersweet memories for me. Memories of the night I had given her the ring and we lay and talked about our dreams, and the sex we'd had out under the stars.

I waved to two of the guys who were just pulling out and backed down the driveway. I climbed into my truck and looked at the new house that stood before me. This was just another chapter I could close on the doors of Jessica.

It had been eight long, grueling months since Jessica had left. Eight months without so much as a single word to me. I had heard through the grapevine that her parents had finally heard from her and that they now knew where she was. I was going to ask them when I last saw them, but it didn't matter because no matter how much time had passed, I still blamed myself for her leaving. I had replayed the night she broke up with me in my head a thousand times or more during these eight months. It always came down to wondering if I had been more supportive or more open to listening to what she was saying, she might still be here by my side. I carried that guilt on my shoulders every single day. She was gone, and I doubted she would be back.

I stopped and picked up dinner at the little diner in town. I was starving and thought about eating in my car but decided it would be best to head home and relax. I had just pulled away from the curb when my cell phone rang on the seat beside me. I pulled off to the side of the road and answered.

"Ben," my dad's voice came over the speaker, "you got a few minutes, son?"

"Sure thing, Dad. What's up?"

"Are you able to come to the office before you head home?"

My heart sank, but I glanced at my watch and then over at my now rapidly cooling dinner. "Sure thing, Dad."

Twenty minutes later, I walked into Dad's office. I smiled as I saw him sitting behind his computer, his glasses down on the tip of his nose as he looked through a pile of bills that sat in front of him. "Hey, Pop," I called, grabbing a bottle of water from the little fridge in the corner of his office.

"Hey, take a seat, would you."

I sat down across from my dad and cracked the bottle of water, drinking down the cool liquid. Anything to quell the pangs of hunger.

"One of the guys mentioned that you are looking to get out of here. Is that true?"

I blew out a breath. I had mentioned nothing to my father. I didn't want to disappoint him or make him think I was unhappy working for him. Truth was, it wasn't the job. I loved the job. It was this town; I needed out. Everywhere I looked there were memories of Jessica. The movie theater, restaurants, even the bloody mall, and all those memories just added to the guilt I still carried. I avoided my father's eyes, even though I knew he would understand. "Sort of," I mumbled.

My dad sat back in his chair and looked me over. "I really count on you, you know. You've become an integral part of this company, taking on projects to free me up to scout out other ones. You've taken on more responsibility even on the business side in the last little while. Are you not enjoying working for me anymore?"

This was the exact reason I hadn't mentioned anything to him. That was the last thing I wanted him to think. "No, Dad, that's not it. I just think I need to get out of this town. Clear my head a bit, you know."

My father looked at me and set the bills aside. "I'm sure this has something to do with Jessica. I get it, I do. After your mom left, I needed to get out of here too. But running from your problems doesn't fix them. I know you know that. Instead, I threw myself into this company and into work, and soon I forgot all about her."

"I know, Dad. You've always taught me that. I think I just need a break. Clear my head so I can look at everything with fresh eyes."

"I understand, and I guess we are coming into the slower season. Let me think about things, see if we can't come up with something. We can talk in the morning. Sound good?"

I nodded and pulled my aching, dirty body out of the chair. Talking in the morning was better than arguing about it tonight. I climbed into my car, took a bite of my cold burger, and put the car into reverse.

The next morning, I pulled into the parking lot extra early. Dad had called me late in the evening and told me he had an extra project on the other side of town and wanted me to lead. He'd promised that this project would be the first that I would not involve him in. With the plans in hand, I left the office to go over things with my crew when I heard my father's voice behind me.

"Ben, can I see you for a second?"

I turned and glanced at my father, his face long. I frowned and followed him into his office. "What is it? Something wrong?"

"Look, I debated telling you about this last night, but I wanted to think on it first. We have an opportunity to bid on a project in Las Vegas. It's a bit of a drive, and at first I was just going to go myself, but after our talk last night, I think this might be the break you need."

"Las Vegas?"

"Yeah, Vegas. So, basically, I will give you the opportunity to bid on this project. I'll send you out there, all expenses paid, and I want you to take this time to clear your head. Then when you come back, I want you refreshed. You have five days."

"Okay, so I bid on this project, then what? Do we send a crew all the way out there if we get it?"

"If you get it, we'll cross that bridge when we come to it. But if it's a good enough deal then, perhaps, I'll back you so you can start your own division of the company out there. Really, son, the opportunities could be endless, and it could be the leg we've been looking for to expand Sunset Builders."

I looked at my father, who now sat there with a smile on his face. It was like a gift from the heavens, for both of us. He had been wanting to expand, and I had been praying for a chance to get out of here. I had gone home last night and prayed for something to come my way.

"I won't disappoint you." I nodded.

"You could never disappoint me, son. Ever. You've worked hard, you've proved yourself to me, and I am thrilled to be handing you this responsibility."

It had been close to a month since I had returned from putting the bid in on the job in Vegas. I had asked my father more than once if he had heard anything, but he assured me that these things took time. Instead, I'd thrown myself into the project I'd been put in charge of and tried to accept the fact that perhaps I hadn't been aggressive enough, or too aggressive with bidding on that project and that I would have to wait for the next one to come in.

It was Friday afternoon, and I stood reading over the revised set of blueprints that had come in for the project we had been working on. Jules sat behind the counter printing off customer invoices, and we both looked up when my father walked in and headed straight toward his office without a word to either of us. He slammed the door and picked up the phone on his desk.

My father's voice started getting elevated, and I feared it was about the job in Vegas. I knew I hadn't done a good enough job to win the bid. As my father yelled, the guys who were in on break cleared the room, and I rolled up the set of prints and shoved them back into our filing system, getting ready to leave too. I was just about to walk out the door when my father's office door opened.

"There you are. Got a second?" he asked, running his hand over his beard.

"Yep." I glanced at Jules, who immediately turned her attention back to the computer.

I followed him back into his office and waited while Dad took a seat behind his desk. He looked down at a piece of paper in front of him, running his hand over his beard again. Something was wrong. I'd blown it; he was pissed.

"Shut the door would yah," he barked. "And take a seat." He nodded at the chair across from where he sat.

I did as he asked, preparing for the trouble I was almost sure was coming my way. The last guy who got called into my father's office and had been told to shut the door got his walking papers the next day. Would my father do that to me if I had botched this deal in Vegas? I prayed not.

I sat there waiting for him to speak, my stomach flopping.

"So, that project in Vegas," he began.

I closed my eyes and held my breath. "What about it?" I questioned.

"Well, I finally heard from them earlier today. I'll admit, I lied to you. Projects never take that long to get back to their contractors."

I closed my eyes. I hadn't gotten it, and I'd failed my father. Fear crept up in me as he made eye contact with me. Normally, I could read him, but not this time, there was nothing that gave away what he was thinking.

"It seems that they liked you. They were more than

happy with the quote you provided, and they have accepted your proposal."

My jaw dropped open. I couldn't believe what I was hearing. "Really?" I could hear the disbelief and excitement in my voice at the same time.

"Yep, they have asked you to start next month."

I stared at my father. "What about the project I'm working on? I can't just walk off that job."

"Ben, I can put John in charge of that one. If you really want out of this town, you need to decide what you want to do. They will not wait forever. You either take it or they will give it to someone else."

I couldn't stop the excitement rising in me at the thought of getting out of this town. "I'll take it then."

"Yes, I know that, but I want to know if it's a temporary thing or if you will consider opening up a new branch of Sunset Builders."

I smiled, and without question, I immediately knew what I wanted. "Let's open up that new division."

A huge smile landed on my father's face, and the next thing I knew, he held his large hand out over his desk for me to shake. I placed my hand in his. "Congratulations!"

Chapter Six

JESSICA - PRESENT DAY

I looked in the mirror and saw a girl that I barely recognized anymore. "How did you get here?" I muttered to myself and picked up the pressed powder compact that sat on the bathroom vanity. I ran the sponge-like pad through the concealer and dabbed at the now bluish-green bruise that was forming nicely on my cheek, courtesy of Kendrick.

I had done everything that my husband had asked of me. I worked hard to get myself in shape, and maintained it. I sat through countless boring parties hoping that just once he would introduce me to the powers that be to make my career take off, like he'd promised. I hung off his arm when asked and stepped away when asked. It was like I was some prize he had won, and I'd done it for years, but there were never the introductions he had promised. Instead, the few contracts I had managed to sign on my own had dropped me after they found out he was the one representing me. By then it was too late; we were married and now I was merely a pawn in his game. I made him look better to the people he deemed important--the ones who still lined his pockets.

As for all the other promises that he had made to me, and occasionally still made, not one of them had come true. He had played a good game and held it long enough to get me to move here with him, into his condo. Now it was too late. I wore his ring—or handcuff as I frequently called it—and he controlled everything. All that ring had really become was a reminder to me of the trap I had fallen into and how naive I'd been to believe it. I looked down at the gold band and cringed.

I once again dabbed at the bruise. We'd had a fight. Kendrick had a meeting this morning, and while I was cooking breakfast, he was sitting in the dining room going over his documents.

With plates in hand, I made my way into the dining room when my foot got caught in the strap of his bag. The glass of orange juice was the first to go, spilling all over the documents on the table.

"You stupid bitch!" he'd yelled, picking up the glass and throwing it across the room. It hit the wall, smashing into a million pieces.

I shook in terror and watched as the plate slipped from my hand, spilling his breakfast all over the remaining documents, and that was when he had backhanded me across the face, knocking me to the floor. As I lay there crying, he gathered his juice-soaked and food-covered documents, shoving them into the garbage. Leaving me on the floor, he took his bag and slammed the condo door.

I shook at the most recent memory. I drew in a breath and gathered my overly processed, dry hair and threw it up into a ponytail and walked into the kitchen. I needed to get out of this relationship. Aside from the constant verbal and physical abuse, I'd had an inkling that Kendrick had been seeing someone else while on his lengthy business trips.

Last year, I had begun to stash money in a hidden cookie jar and stored it in the back of one of the kitchen cupboards. Kendrick never lifted a finger in the kitchen. In fact, I was sure he had never even stepped into this one, so I knew the money was safe there.

I climbed onto a chair and pulled the jar down from the back of the cupboard. I placed it on the counter and lifted the lid and pulled out a roll of bills. I reached into my pocket and quickly added sixty dollars that was left over from the money Kendrick had given me earlier in the week for groceries, and replaced the lid, then I climbed back up on the chair and put the cookie jar back.

I was surprised at the amount I'd been able to save. The way Kendrick tracked my spending, it was a wonder I could save anything at all. He gave me just enough money every month to buy my personal care items and our groceries, and demanded receipts for everything I'd buy. However, as the abuse got worse, I started looking for ways to cut. Instead of using premium lines of care products, I started buying cheaper products and refilling the bottles of the premium lines when Kendrick wasn't home so I didn't give it away that I had switched anything. I also started shopping for food that was on sale or clearance, enabling me to save even more. Most of the time I'd lie and say I'd lost the receipt or that the cashier must not have placed it in the grocery bag as I'd asked her. He'd huff and puff and bark at me, but it had been worth it. It would only be a matter of time before I could leave. Once I'd put the chair back, I headed down to the lobby of the condo to get the mail.

I nodded at the doorman and pulled open the little mailbox. It was part of my daily routine to get the mail, and I pulled out a large stack and went back upstairs. Once inside the condo, I sifted through the mail, all of it for Kendrick, but the last piece caught my eye. My name was on the legal-sized manila envelope, the return address from Malone Family Law Firm, Kings Cove Harbor. I frowned as I turned the envelope over in my hands.

I sat down at the kitchen table and opened the envelope and read the letter inside. I'd barely made it past the first couple of sentences when tears quickly clouded my vision. My grandfather, James McKay, had passed away over four months ago. Growing up, I had been very close to my grandfather, and after he'd had a falling out with my mother, he had moved away. I could remember going to spend summers with him in Kings Cove Harbor when I was little, and I wiped the tears from my eyes and did my best to concentrate on the letter.

"James McKay has named you as sole beneficiary of his estate. Please contact me to discuss transfer of property located at 2501-425 Las Vegas Boulevard, and all financial accounts."

I covered my mouth and squealed with excitement. I re-read the letter again before folding it up and placing it in my pocket. This was my ticket out of here. I couldn't help but feel my excitement build. I glanced at the clock on the stove. It was Wednesday and almost ten. I had to meet Kate for our usual coffee date.

I walked by the window of our usual meeting place and saw Kate sitting at a table waiting for me.

"Morning!" I greeted as I approached the table.

"Morning," she said, looking up from her favorite gossip rag *Everyday Celebrity*. "My God, what the hell happened to you?" she questioned, closing the magazine and reaching out to touch my cheek.

I closed my eyes. I'd thought I'd covered it enough that no one would notice. "Kendrick went on another one of his rampages this morning," I said, ducking out of the way of her touch.

"Oh, Jessica, I so wish you had taken my advice all those years ago. He's put his hands on you too many times. You need to get out of there."

"Yes, I know. The good news is I think I may have found a way to be able to leave."

"Oh?"

"Yes! Thanks to this little gem that arrived this morning, I now have a place to go, a place Kendrick won't know about," I said, pulling the letter from my back pocket and handing it to Kate for her to read.

She opened it and read the letter twice, and then looked at me and smiled. "Amazing!"

"Yes, it's almost like a dream come true. The only thing is that I don't know how I will get there. I mean, you know the short leash Kendrick keeps me on. There is no way he will let me go willingly, and I can't exactly run. He'll find me."

Kate sat there sipping on her coffee, looking off into the distance as I told her more about the place I had inherited. As I rambled on, she finally met my eyes, a smile coming to her lips.

"What if I told you I would take you to Vegas?"

"Kate, I can't ask you to put yourself in harm's way."

"Harm's way? Girl, I am not afraid of Kendrick. Besides, doesn't he have a trip coming up?"

"Yes, don't remind me. Four or five weeks this time, and I know damn well that he's shacking up with another woman," I bit out.

"So let him shack up. What do you care?"

"I only care because I don't know what diseases he is bringing home to me."

"True. Look, don't give it a second thought. We'll leave in the late-morning after Kendrick has left for the airport. He'll be gone for four weeks at least. By the time he gets home, we will be long gone. I have a photo shoot out there anyway."

"I don't know, Kate. What if I'm wrong about the other women or he ends up wanting me to go with him? He never normally leaves me alone for that length of time."

"Fake the flu. He won't want you around when you're sick, that much I know."

I let out a laugh. "Yeah, you're right."

"All right, so it's settled. Write that letter, contact that lawyer, and let's go. It will be one big, tremendous adventure."

Later that afternoon, I sat in Kendrick's office, behind his over-sized oak desk, with a piece of paper and pen in front of me. I'd called Malone Family Law and spoke with Hunter Malone, and then I took my time writing out the letter I intended to send. I re-read the words I had written and then signed the papers he had sent. I took the sealed envelope and went into the kitchen to grab the cookie jar from the cupboard. I grabbed a few dollars from my savings and slid it back into the cupboard.

Kendrick would be home in forty minutes, and I needed to get this letter sent before he returned. I rushed down to the post office, paid for the registered letter to be delivered overnight, and then made my way back to our condo where I spent the next hour getting dinner ready. I wanted nothing out of place or for Kendrick to suspect anything at all.

Kendrick had come home in an awful, foul mood, and after we had eaten, he sat in the dining room going over his travel details. I was in the kitchen listening to him bark out orders over the phone while I cleaned everything up. I had just put the last of the dishes into the dishwasher and was washing down the counter when I felt his arms slide around my waist.

"So, I leave tomorrow morning. I was thinking perhaps you could join me."

I closed my eyes as his hands traveled down my hips. I said nothing. He hadn't wanted to travel with me in years. It was almost as if he'd known of my plan and was doing this on purpose.

"What if I told you I just booked your flight?" he asked, kissing my neck.

I swallowed hard. Kate had been right. I should have known he would pull this. "Great," I murmured.

"What do you say we crawl into bed?" he

whispered into my ear, his lips grazing along the skin of my neck.

One thing I had learned over the years was never to turn Kendrick away. If I did, it would just lead to another fight, and it was another argument I already knew he wouldn't let me win. Without hesitation, I put the cloth I held in my hand down and allowed Kendrick to lead me to the bedroom.

I woke to the sound of Kendrick smashing things around in the bathroom as he got ready for his day. I rolled onto my back and flung my arm over my eyes. The bathroom door opened, and he marched into the bedroom and growled my name. "Jessica, get up, we'll be late. The car will be here in ten minutes to take us to the airport."

I curled into a tight ball and held onto my stomach, moaning in fake pain.

"What is with you? Come on and get up."

"I was up all night sick, Kendrick," I cried.

"Jessica, stop this nonsense. Get up. Your flight is non-refundable. I'm not in the practice of giving flights away," he barked as he grabbed his suitcase.

"Kendrick, don't you understand that I'm sick. I can't go."

I could tell he was furious without even looking at him. I could feel his eyes drilling into me as I lay there.

"Don't ever ask me for another trip again," he barked, and began stomping around the room.

I lay in the fetal position while Kendrick packed. Once he was out of the room, I heard him on his phone, and I strained to hear. He would be picking someone up shortly, and was asking that my name be switched off the ticket and be placed in another name, only I couldn't make out the name he'd said. Minutes later, the condo door slammed shut, and once I was sure he wasn't coming back, I jumped out of bed and got dressed, pulling my already packed bag out from under the bed. Then I headed for the kitchen. Climbing on the stool, I reached into the back of the cupboard and emptied the cookie jar. I placed some money into my wallet, and the rest I slid into an old envelope and into my suitcase. I then went back into the bedroom and went back through another one of my packed duffel bags. I needed to decide what would come with me and what would stay. If I took everything, he would know I'd left. This way, once he returned, he would think I had just gone out for the night.

I took one last look around the condo I had grown to hate and zipped up the bag. I looked down at my left hand and pulled at the wedding band. I wanted to get this ring off, and with a little soap and water, it finally slid off with ease. I set it in a ring dish that Kendrick probably didn't even know we had on top of my dresser.

I called Kate as soon as I left the condo, and by the time I was down on the sidewalk, I only waited for a few seconds until she pulled up to the curb in her car exactly as planned. I threw my bags into the back seat and climbed in. Kate pulled away from the curb. I didn't even look behind me as we sped away from the building. My life now only sat ahead. Behind was over.

Chapter Seven

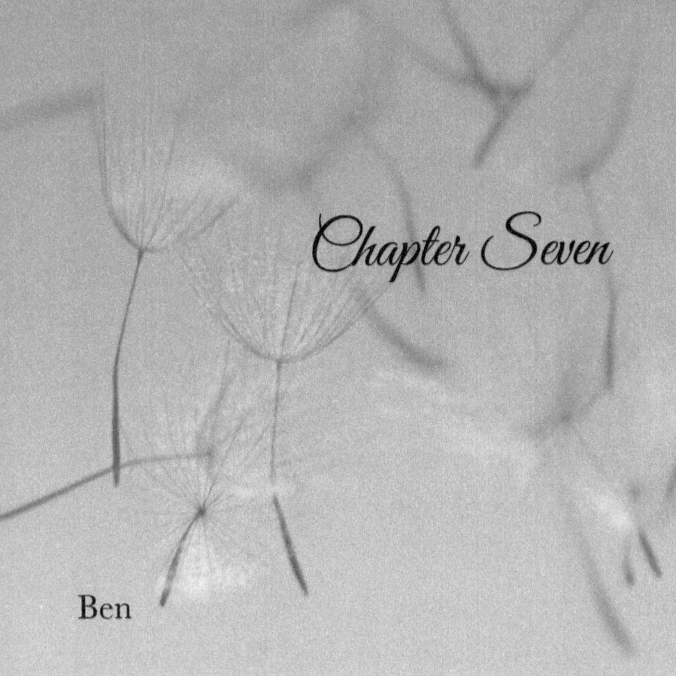

Ben

The days were getting longer as summer neared. Things were finally picking up. We had scheduled five projects in the past week. The increase in work had left me feeling exhausted. I was glad it was Friday, and I was looking forward to that cold beer, only I knew this one would taste better than last Friday's. I had to finish one final appointment and then stop into the office before I started home. A cold beer and the start of my long-awaited vacation were calling me.

It was a little past three when I marked off the last section of the checklist for the job we had just spent the last year and a half at. It had finally been completed, and I stood in front of a beautiful home and a very thrilled couple. I traded Mr. King the keys to their new home for my pen and the release documents he'd just signed.

"I hope that we have met your expectations," I said, smiling.

"Ben, you have done a wonderful job. Anna and I are both thrilled. If only your father could see what you have done. He would be so proud. You've kept his vision and the core values of Sunset Builders and never strayed."

I immediately remembered the words my father told me the day we opened this division. *"Make sure that you always leave the customers with a smile on their face. If you can do that, you will succeed."* I valued those words to this day, and always strived to make my father the happiest he could be, even though he had handed my sister, Jules, and me complete control over the entire company three years ago when he was diagnosed with cancer.

I nodded. "I am glad that you are satisfied with everything. If you need anything else, if anything needs touching up, call the office. Julie will get you booked, and I will make sure someone is out as soon as possible."

"Thanks, Ben. I will send some recommendations your way. We have a few friends looking to get some work done." Mr. King shook my hand, and I climbed into the driver's seat of my truck. Mrs. King waved as I backed out of their driveway.

It took me a half an hour to get back to the office. I parked my truck in my usual spot and grabbed the Kings' file from the front passenger's seat. I climbed the stairs to the office door and walked into the cool air. It didn't matter how long I had been working in the city, I still wasn't and never would be used to the dreaded city heat.

I dropped the signed documents on Julie's desk and removed all the mail from my mail cubby. I opened the door to my office and sat down behind my desk, beginning to weed out the junk from the pile of items that were actually important. The Kings' project had been the biggest renovation this division of Sunset Builders had done. Even though I was excited to start my next project, I was also itching for some rest and relaxation. I flipped on my computer screen and was greeted with the view of the lake that my cottage sat on--a view I was looking forward to visiting next week.

I opened the first piece of mail that sat on top of the pile when Julie, my sister and office manager, came flying into my office. She sifted through the pile of papers on my desk, removing two invoices that were buried.

"I wasn't expecting you to be back here so early this afternoon."

"Well, I turned the keys over to Mr. King. It is Friday, so I thought I would bring you the signed documents along with their final payment so you could get it into the bank. It was too far to drive out to some other renovations locations. Plus, it's the start of my vacation, in case you've forgotten. Oh, and I left the Kings' file on your desk."

She looked at me and shook her head, knowing that the excuse of it being too far to drive was exactly that, an excuse. I could tell she was about to rip me a new one for being lazy when the phone rang.

"Whatever. Oh, don't go anywhere. Just give me a second," Julie said, darting out of my office, running to grab the ringing phone. I chuckled to myself, watching as my sister flew around the reception desk and grabbed the phone.

I set aside the mail and pulled up a map while Jules' voice murmured in the background. Trying not to listen I focused on trying to find the best route to take to the cottage. I glanced up from my monitor to see Julie taking down some notes. I was about to go back to studying the map when I heard my name and then saw her hesitating to book an appointment. I frowned, watching as she briefly made eye contact with me, then turned around and assured the person on the other side of the phone that someone would be there tomorrow morning.

I gritted my teeth as she hung up the phone and began walking toward my office. I had a feeling I knew what was coming. Seconds later, with her hands behind her back, she came wandering back into my office and sat down across from me. "What you doing?" she sang with curiosity in her voice.

"I'm planning my route. I'm just trying to figure out the quickest and easiest way to get there without stressing myself out. You know, to beat all the traffic," I said, glancing at her. She sat there with an odd smile on her face. "What?" I questioned. I knew that something was up, and I had a feeling that I was not going to like what she was going to tell me.

"About your vacation..."

I shook my head. "Oh no. Come on, Jules, it's been three years since I got away. I just finished an immense job, and between running this office and making weekly visits to the other one, I'm burnt out. One week. It's only one week. That's all I want," I said, sitting back and running my hands through my hair.

"I know, I know. How about after this one you can go?" she said, grinning.

I sat back and blew out a breath. "You know as well as I do that will not happen. I'll get sucked into something else and be screwed, and the next thing I know it will be another three years," I bit out, putting my hands behind my head as I watched the week of solitude I'd been looking forward to disappear before me.

Jules looked at me, a slight smile on her face while her eyes pleaded with me.

I let out a sigh. "What do you know about the project?" I questioned, reaching for a pencil.

"Okay, okay, I am so excited. So, it's a kitchen and double bathroom renovation. It's a new owner, and she wants to upgrade to sell."

"All right." I scribbled down what Jules had just told me.

"Yes, and since she is selling, she expressed that there'd be no expense spared."

I chuckled under my breath. "Ya, I've heard that before, then they get my estimate and go with someone half my price," I mumbled. "What's the address?"

"Half the price and half the quality, remember that."

"Yeah, yeah. What's the address?"

"Are you ready?" She sat there grinning at me like a fool. Either the place was nice or it was a complete dump.

"Julie, just tell me," I barked.

"Gee, someone's grumpy this afternoon."

"Julie..." I gritted.

"Fine, it's 2501-425 Las Vegas Boulevard."

I wrote as she said the address and then glanced up at her. "You serious?"

"You heard me. You really need to go bid on this. Getting into that area of Vegas would be amazing."

Without wasting another minute, I reached into my desk and pulled out my portfolio, my measuring tape, and my sample kit, and stood up, shutting off the screen on my computer. I had been trying to get into that area of the city for three years. "All right, I'm out of here. As for you, all I will say is that if I am skipping vacation, then I better be home tonight in time to watch the Vegas Knights play."

"You'll be fine. The game isn't on until nine, it's only four." Julie waved as I walked out the door. "Go get 'em!"

"Oh, and who am I seeing?"

"Ah, Kate, a Kate Green."

"Good afternoon, sir," I heard as I approached the large double doors of 425 Las Vegas Boulevard.

"Afternoon." I glanced down at the name tag the gentleman wore. "Jon."

"Welcome to 425 Las Vegas Boulevard, sir."

"Thank you, Jon. I'm here to see someone in apartment 2501."

"Ah, yes, Mr. McKay. Wonderful gentleman, although I haven't seen him in a while. Very well, sir."

I frowned. Perhaps Kate Green was a personal friend, I thought to myself as I entered through the door and walked across the plush carpeting of the lobby. I probably should have worn shoes and not work boots that had been caked in mud, I thought to myself as I looked back and noticed a small trail of mud crumbs. I pressed the button for the elevator and stood there looking around while I waited.

The ding of the elevator tore me from my thoughts, and as the door opened, I went to walk in but stopped in my tracks. Doug Dixon, center for the Vegas Knights, stood in front of me. I could barely believe my eyes. I was a huge fan of his, and I could tell the second that he looked at me he knew it.

"Hey, man, afternoon," he mumbled as he stepped out of the elevator and continued by me.

"Afternoon," I mumbled, completely shocked at

seeing him. I watched as he walked out of the lobby, and that was when I noticed the doors of the elevator starting to close. I quickly stuck my arm between them and stepped into the elevator, pressing the 25th floor button.

Chapter Eight

JESSICA

I was already sick and tired of having contractors traipse through the place. I'd had Kate's help to book all of them to come by today. I'd figured it would be easier that way and take up less of my time since I was on a limited schedule to get everything done. I'd already been living in the apartment for a week, and the longer it took to make my decision, the quicker my time would run out.

I'd needed to live here for a bit to figure out what the place needed before I made any rash decisions and spent money that didn't need to be spent. While the place was in great shape, I wanted to get the most I could for the condo, since I would need that money if I were leaving Kendrick. It hadn't taken me long to decide to update the two bathrooms, give everything a fresh coat of paint, and update the kitchen. Kate had also told me that those were the rooms that added the most value.

I glanced at the clock. The last and final contractor would be here soon. I flipped the kettle on and thought back to the last contractor who had been here. He had walked around the place, looking at everything with a slimy smile on his face, his eyes washing over my body every chance he got. I'd had enough of his behavior and was just going to ask him to leave when he turned to me.

"Well, miss, it can be done, with money, of course."

"How much?"

The contractor scribbled a few things down on the lined pad he carried, scratched his beer gut where his shirt kept riding up, and then chuckled to himself. "And you said something about marble countertops, correct?"

"Yes, that is what I said," I answered with a bitchy undertone.

"Well, little lady, as soon as the man of the house is available, we can have the discussion surrounding the price, so why don't you get him, and then we'll have a talk," he said, turning and continuing to look around.

I frowned and grumbled under my breath. "Look, I'm technically not married," I lied. "I inherited this place, and I plan to fix it and flip it. So why don't you just level with me."

He chuckled to himself once again, scribbled something else down on the sheet of paper he had in front of him, and tore it off. He folded it in half and handed it to me, his eyes running over my body. "Let me know," he barked before stomping out of the apartment and slamming the door behind him.

I'd opened the folded paper he'd handed me and looked down at the price he'd written down. I balled up the paper and jumped as the door slammed shut. I was tired of contractors traipsing in here, demanding to talk to my husband, treating me as if I were nothing more than a piece of meat that knew nothing. Why was it that all the men in these trades thought because you had a vagina you weren't capable of making a decision.

I had three quotes, and I reached for the paperwork Hunter Malone had sent me. We had spoken not too long after I'd gotten here. When I told him I was planning on selling the property, he told me that if I invested it right, I would probably be set for life. Then he had told me that he had a tidy sum waiting to be deposited in my account. I had to be careful. Since Kendrick had access to all of my accounts, I couldn't just give Hunter Malone one of my regular accounts. I'd asked that he set up an account for me. He had done so with no questions or arguments, and now I was just waiting for the money to be transferred. I had no clue what the sum of those accounts was, but I'd planned to use that money to do the updating. I'd have to check the bank in the morning, I thought, and closed the file then poured my tea.

I set my mug on the table and then ran my finger across the books on my grandfather's bookshelf. He had quite the extensive collection, and it had been so long since I had read anything.

I remembered as a little girl I would sit with my grandfather while he read. I'd have one of his novels in my lap and I would pretend to read, just like him. Unfortunately, over the years, I had stopped reading because Kendrick thought it was a waste of my time. I ran my fingers over the books again, finally settling on a mystery, and sat down at the dining room table, opening the book. I'd lost track of time and was deep into the fourth chapter when a loud knock pulled me away.

I glanced at the clock. "Finally, the last one." I sighed, closing the book. I walked over, straightening the cushion on the couch on my way, and pulled open the door. His back was to me, but the first thing I noticed were his broad shoulders and tight waist. The second thing was his muscular forearms that held onto a notebook. He turned abruptly and introduced himself, but stopped before he could get his words out.

I glanced up as he'd stopped speaking mid-sentence, his hand out halfway, his eyes meeting mine and washing over me. I'd know those eyes anywhere, and a pang of guilt hit me as I recognized him instantly. Ben. I swallowed hard. I hadn't seen him since the night I'd crawled out of his car in tears. The night I left home.

He looked just like I remembered: dark-brown hair, deep chestnut eyes, strong chiseled features, more bulk than I remembered, and only a little older. I sucked in a deep breath. "Ben?" His name felt so familiar on my lips, as if I had never stopped saying it.

"Jess?" He swallowed hard, and he quickly retracted his hand and shoved it deep into his pocket. He blinked hard, and for two seconds, we just stood there looking at one another. A door down the hall slammed shut, pulling me out of my thoughts.

"Come on in. Please," I said, stepping off to the side, making room for him to enter.

He walked by me, and I shut the door. Now he

stood across from me in my apartment. We looked at one another, neither of us saying anything. It felt like we had been standing there forever when Ben finally cleared his throat. "So, you need some work done? You need a quote?"

It was as if I had forgotten the reason he was there. I felt my face heat, and I cleared my throat. "Yes. Um, sorry, you were probably expecting a Kate Green. She's a close friend," I muttered, looking around the apartment like I'd forgotten the question he'd asked. "Ah, yes, both bathrooms and the kitchen need renovating, and a coat of fresh paint through the entire place," I said, first looking at him and then leading him down the hall to the first bathroom.

I couldn't help but watch him as he went straight to work, drawing out the room on a piece of paper, taking measurements and marking them down. I remembered watching him when he had first started working with his dad. I could remember the concentration on his face as he would practice doing quotes for his father's company. He even used the exact same methods and still had the same cute, concentrated look on his face now. I smiled at the memory. I had spent many weekends by his side then.

A half hour later, when the bathroom drawings were complete, we stood across from one another in the kitchen. I could tell he was doing his best to avoid eye contact as he set his pad down on the counter and walked through the kitchen. "So tell me, what were your thoughts for the kitchen?"

I shrugged. I had given little thought to it, especially after seeing what he had proposed for the bathrooms, everything so different from what I had originally thought about. "I guess I just want to update it—nothing major. I like the openness to it."

"Yes, I love the open concept. Plus, the view is amazing to look out over the city as you cook, I bet," he said, walking behind the counter and looking across the living room out the floor-to-ceiling windows. "Nice and bright in here too."

"Yes, it is."

He reached for his paper and began writing out some things while I went over and grabbed my tea.

"So what are you planning to do with the place after the renovations?" he questioned, starting to work on another drawing.

"My grandfather passed away and left me the place. I don't really need it, so I plan on flipping it."

"Sorry to hear about your grandfather," Ben said, continuing to make notes as he studied the lighting in the ceiling. "Do you like the pot lights?" he questioned.

"Sure, they provide enough light," I said, looking up at them. I cleared my throat. "So, your dad finally branched out and grew the business, did he?" I questioned, while Ben continued making more notes.

"Yeah, originally, but now it's mine."

"Wow, congratulations! That must have been a big step, taking over the business."

"It was, but I didn't have much choice. When Dad died of cancer, I didn't have many options. It was keep it or sell it. So I run both locations now."

"I'm sorry to hear about your father," I bit out, suddenly feeling uncomfortable.

Ben shrugged. "Thanks." A look of pain came over his face.

I had to change the subject. I didn't know how sick his dad had gotten, but I sensed it was bad, judging from the look on Ben's face. "So, what made you originally decide to open a location all the way out here?"

Ben stopped writing and looked up at me, his expression going from familiar and friendly to utterly intense. I'd seen that look in his eyes before, and the second his dark eyes hit mine, I felt that familiar feeling in my stomach, the same one I had gotten the night I had told him about my opportunity. "Needed a change of pace, I guess. You know how that is," he gritted out.

I flinched at his comment. Those were the same words I had once used. I knew damn well those words were directed toward me, but I tried hard not to let it get to me. "I'm glad that you've done well for yourself."

Ben cleared his throat and put his pencil down. "Why don't you flip through these sample books and tell me your choices," he said, handing over the book.

I hesitantly started flipping through the books, making some choices and trying to envision what it all would look like changed, while Ben continued taking measurements. Once I had picked some things out, I pointed to each of the samples I liked and Ben nodded, making his notes.

"All right, well, let me know once your husband is home and we can discuss pricing," he said, looking down to my left hand where the indent from my wedding ring was still prevalent.

I covered my hand and looked at Ben. "I'm not technically married, so you can just leave me the quote. I'll be the one taking care of this." I was about to branch out into a deeper explanation I felt that I perhaps owed him when he held up his hand, stopping me.

"Hey, no need to explain. I really don't care either way. Leave it with me. I will get you a quote in two days." Ben grabbed his belongings, and I walked him to the door. "I can reach you at the number you gave my office?" he questioned, glancing down again at the notes.

"Yep."

We stood there in awkward silence, looking at one another. Then he stepped forward. "It was nice to see you, Jess," he said, leaning in and giving me an awkward hug.

"You too." I smiled, trying hard to keep my composure. "I look forward to your call."

Seconds later, he pulled the door open, and I watched Ben as he walked down the hall, not turning to look back. I watched as he stood at the elevator, and I stayed there watching until the doors to the elevator shut. Then I shut and locked the apartment door and walked back over to the dining room table. In a matter of a half an hour, I had gone from getting quotes from annoying contractors to once again regretting the very day that I got on that bus and left my sleepy little town even more than I already did.

Chapter Nine

Ben

Memories had haunted me all weekend. Memories that I wished my mind had forgotten. Still, after three days, the only image in my mind was the night I had dropped Jessica off at her house. I remembered those gorgeous eyes as they filled with tears and the look of hurt that sat on her face and in her eyes because of me. All because I hadn't been able to give her room to breathe. All because I couldn't understand her need for something more. The more I thought about it, the more that feeling crept over me as it had that night, and for the past five years.

I was glad that the office was quiet because my

concentration was all over the place. I sat staring at the mess of numbers on my screen, not really seeing any of them. I had been trying to make sense of everything for the entire weekend. Had she looked me up and known that this was my company? Was this some sly way of getting back at me for what happened between us all those years ago? Was I going to do all this work for her to shove the quote back in my face. Surely, she wouldn't have called me out of spite. I shoved that thought out of my mind. I was being silly. However, I feared that our past probably would have a direct impact on whether I got this job. That much, I was sure of.

I ran my hand through my hair and blew out a frustrated breath. I should have been at my cottage. I should be sitting in my boat on the lake, my fishing line in the water. I should be having a peaceful day out on the lake and bringing back fresh fish for dinner. Instead, here I sat after a weekend of not being able to get her off my mind, more wound up than I had been on Friday, struggling over how the hell to price a job. It would have been better if I had handed off the pricing job to Julie or one of the other guys, I thought as I typed in the wrong figure and then erased it.

Frustrated, I stood up to grab a bottle of water from the fridge and dug my hand into my pocket and instantly grabbed hold of the item that always rested there. I held onto that tiny circular item and sat back down at my desk, once again hitting the calculator.

"Oh my God, tell me you aren't playing with that thing again?" Julie asked from the doorway, laughing.

I rolled my eyes. I'd figured she was long gone by now, not standing here skulking around watching me. It was already late. I gripped the ring I'd pinned to the inside of my pocket. It was the same ring that I had given to Jess all those years ago, and I clenched it in the palm of my hand. "Hilarious, Jules. Just fucking hilarious."

She leaned up against the doorway, studying me. "What are you working on that's got you in such a mood? It's almost time to go."

"Working on that quote. You know, the one that took away my week of solitude," I said, slamming the keys of the calculator again, trying to be as competitive as I could be.

"I see," Julie mumbled and sat down across from me, taking in what I was sure were worry lines on my face. "Is it a problem with what the person wants?" she said, reaching for my paperwork and looking over the list of items I was pricing.

I let out a huff as I once again made a mistake on the calculator, causing me to look up at her. Irritated, I mumbled, "No, it's not that." I paused.

"Then what is it?"

"You'll never guess who I saw today."

"The Pope?" Julie said mockingly, putting her feet up on the edge of my desk.

I clenched my jaw and gave her annoyed look.

"Jesus, you're so sensitive today. You know I'm just trying to make you laugh," she said as she rolled her eyes. "Anyways, Mr. Sensitive, who did you see?"

"Jess," I bit out, completely frustrated.

I heard the soft inhale from Julie and looked up. Judging from the look on her face, I was glad she was sitting down. She gripped the edge of my desk and sat forward. "Whoa! Tell me EVERYTHING! You can't hold back ANYTHING! When, where, how did she look? Did you talk to her?"

"Funny, the look on your face is probably the same one I had when she answered the door."

"Answered the door? What door?"

"Oh yeah, did I forget to mention that she is the owner of the apartment on Las Vegas Boulevard, not Kate Green? Again, the one you made me miss vacation for."

Jules sat there chewing on her thumb. "I'm sorry. So how did she look?" she questioned then sat there waiting for me to continue.

"She looks sad, Jules, and thin, so thin. She was jumpy, or maybe the correct term was on edge, and I noticed a hint of a bruise on her cheek," I whispered, the thought of how she got it filling me with an unsettling feeling.

"What did she say when she saw you?"

"Not much. She asked me questions about the business, when I branched out."

"Let me guess, you were your normal charming self, weren't you?"

"Hey, I just told her the truth."

"So you were a prick instead?" Jules questioned. When I didn't answer, she swallowed hard and kept questioning me. "Is she married?"

"Well, her answer to that was 'not technically,' whatever that means."

Julie thought for a moment and looked at me. "Perhaps it's a fresh separation? You know, the wound is still open." She shrugged.

"Perhaps. All I know is that it was simply weird. It was like she got pissed at me when I mentioned her husband."

"She sounds like someone has hurt her. Perhaps he wasn't a nice guy, maybe that's why she didn't elaborate. Did you talk about anything else?"

"No, nothing major. She told me that her grandfather just passed, so perhaps that was why she was acting weird. She was really close to him when we were younger."

"Maybe, or perhaps your reading way too far into

it, and it was because she landed her eyes on your ugly mug."

"Haha, you're funny." I stood up and reached into my jeans pocket, grabbing the ring. It only took me a second, and I unpinned the pin and dropped the ring onto my desktop.

"What is that?" Julie asked, reaching for the mess of string, while I walked over to the coffeemaker to pour us the last two cups of coffee in the pot.

"<u>That</u> is the ring I proposed to Jess with all those years ago."

I glanced over and watched as she picked up the ring and looked at it and then looked to me. "You mean you've carried this in your pocket all this time? Here I thought you were just incapable of leaving your member alone." She giggled.

"Fuck, you just think you're hilarious don't you?"

"There was a time you did think so," she said, still looking at the ring.

I dropped two spoonfuls of sugar into my mug and one into Jules', then stirred them and carried them over to the desk, setting one in front of Julie. I took a seat and nodded. "To answer your question, yes, ever since she left it sitting in the palm of my hand, it has been on that string inside my jean pocket."

Jules kept her eyes trained on the ring and whispered, "Why?"

I shrugged. "I don't know. I guess I hoped that one day she would come back and claim it." I was sure I sounded pathetic to my sister. Hell, I sounded pathetic even to myself. I'd spent the better part of my life wanting someone to come back, when she was off not even thinking of me.

Chapter Ten

JESSICA

The rain had woken me early this morning, and now I padded across the plush carpet in my bare feet, carrying a hot cup of coffee, and sat down on the couch. I had to get ready to meet Kate for lunch in a little bit and just wanted to take a few moments to relax. I grabbed my phone and refreshed my email.

It surprised me to see two new emails appear in my inbox. The first was from Hunter Malone, letting me know that half of the funds had been transferred and should now be available in my new account. The second was from Ben, the subject line titled "quote." My stomach turned as I opened it. I was disappointed that he hadn't written anything, but had just attached the quote, but upon second thought, it surprised me he had even sent it. I really hadn't expected to hear from him, but like clockwork, the quote appeared.

The look of shock on his face when I had opened the door and he had seen me for the first time was still fresh in my mind. At first, things were super awkward. I'd always wondered what it would be like for us to run into one another again. It didn't shock me that things had been awkward at first, and as I had watched him work, I figured that perhaps I would be able to hire him for the job. However, as time wore on, the more we talked, the more he became cold and short-tempered.

I clicked on the attachment and looked over the quote he had sent, noticing that it was significantly higher than the others. Frustrated, I put my phone down. I had no clue what or whom to choose. I would have Kate look these over with me during lunch. I was sure she would help me decide; she had more of a business sense than I did. We were meeting at Sinatra, some weird fusion restaurant not too far from here. I wasn't overly thrilled about meeting in public. It was just an excuse to eat lunch because we were only going to be talking about the construction quotes. She could have just as easily come here for coffee. I got up, drank down the last of my coffee, and headed to the bathroom for a shower.

I sat with my face in the menu, trying to decide what to eat for lunch. Kate sat there sipping on her Bellini, deeply sighing at the fact that in twenty minutes I still hadn't decided on anything. With the next loud exhale, I shut my menu and looked over at her. "Sorry, I'm just not all that hungry for weird food."

Kate let out a loud laugh. "Okay, how about we just order a bunch of tapas and share then?"

"Sounds good, I guess." I pulled my phone from my purse and pulled up the quotes and slid my phone over to her.

"Oh, the quotes! Let me see," she said, rubbing her hands together and going over the first one.

Two of the quotes had come in fairly close to one another, and then there was Ben's. I'd given it some thought. Even though it was the highest of them all, for some reason it didn't bother me because I knew he wouldn't screw me. I watched Kate as her eyes skimmed over each of them while sipping on her Bellini until the glass was empty.

"So what do you think?" I asked, taking a sip of my martini.

"First things first, I need another drink." She giggled while waving the waitress over to our table and ordering another drink. "Okay, so, what I really want to know is which of these contractors is the cutest?"

I rolled my eyes and set my glass back down. "What does cute have to do with it, Kate? They are coming in and ripping my place apart. That's it, that's all."

Kate chuckled to herself. "Well, my dear, you are single, in case I needed to remind you."

"You don't need to remind me, and I am not single. I'm not even in the process of a separation. I've left him, he doesn't know it yet. The last thing I need is another man."

Kate waved me off as if I were just being silly. "Well, if you will be stuck inside of your place all day with dirty, sweaty men, which honestly doesn't sound all that bad if you ask me, you definitely want a buff guy walking around your apartment. You know, shirtless, with abs, and whatever those drive-us-wild lines are called peeking out the top of his low-slung jeans." She winked and took a sip of the drink the waitress had just dropped off at the table.

The first two contractors had been about fifteen years older than me, with beer guts and the matching plumber's cracks to go with them. Ben, though, had stayed in shape. I thought of the way his T-shirt had snuggly hugged his broad shoulders, and how it stretched across his back and biceps. If in shape was what she wanted, Ben was it.

"Spill it, girl," Kate said, raising her glass to me. "What's on that mind of yours?"

I smiled. "Well, if we are going purely based on looks, then that would be Ben," I mumbled.

"Ben?"

"Yeah, from Sunset Builders."

Kate shuffled through the quotes again. She glanced at me. "You're on a first-name basis already, after only one meeting? And you say you're not single. Although, need I remind you that his is the highest quote."

"Yes, I know his is the most expensive, and it wasn't exactly our first meeting." I swirled my finger around the top of my glass, eying her reaction.

She studied me, and I could tell she wanted me to elaborate. She didn't wait for me to offer an explanation. "What do you mean it wasn't exactly your first meeting?" she questioned, clearing her throat.

"He asked me to marry him," I said in a barely audible voice.

"TODAY?" Kate asked, sitting forward, waiting for

all the information to pour out. "That's bold, wouldn't you say?"

"No, Kate, not today," I said, rolling my eyes. "If you must know, it would be almost seven years ago now I guess, perhaps longer. We dated in high school and college."

"Ah, uh-huh, the one who got away!" Kate said, giving me a knowing glance.

"No, more like the one I threw away," I said, meeting her eyes.

"All right, so now I am even more curious. Why the hell did you say no?"

I thought back to that night. I could almost put myself right back into the moment, sitting in the front seat of his car as he read over the letter I had received, while I twirled his ring around my finger in excitement. I remembered watching his eyes as he read. I remembered seeing the disappointment, the fear, the unknown in his eyes as I presented him with a ticket to what I was sure would be a better life. I had been so unhappy with everything after we'd graduated, and this had been the one thing that had been able to put a smile on my face for months. I could still feel how badly I had wanted him to say he would move with me. Instead, he got angry and shattered the dream of us within seconds, causing me to run. I'd left behind everything, met Kendrick, and had never returned. I hadn't even gone back to see my parents, and they were long gone now.

"Well..." I blinked away the burning sensation in my eyes. "He'd asked me to marry him about two months earlier to me moving. Things were going well, I had said yes. Then something happened. I started to hate everything that was in my life. I wanted more, I wanted something bigger. I auditioned in the mall one night for the modeling gig. After that, all I could think about was what could be. Things changed between us. I wasn't happy, he wanted things for us that I didn't. Then I received the modeling opportunity."

"Okay, and..."

"I was so excited. I hated living in that town, nothing ever changed. I had dreams, and when I showed him what they had sent me, he burst that dream. He thought it was a silly idea for me to even have entered what he called a cattle call. He thought that following some directions in some silly letter was ridiculous. He was so against the idea. We got into a fight, if you could even call it that. I had wanted him to go with me, he didn't want to leave. He wanted to stay and work for his father and build a family there with me. I got angry, and while he drove me home in silence, a rage filled hatred grew inside of me. When he dropped me off at home, I gave him back his ring. That night, I packed my bags. I thought about not leaving, but I didn't want to see the pain I had caused, and I knew he would come back in the morning and try to make things right. So I ran away from home. I took my offer, walked to the bus station, and bought a ticket, never looking back. That is the man Ben is. In hindsight, he was right, I should have just stayed and not been so trusting. Although he wasn't the only one I hurt. I hurt my parents as well. I never got a chance to say good-bye to either of them before they passed."

"So you left him behind to chase your dreams. There is nothing wrong with that. I would have probably done the same thing."

"Yeah, some dreams. Kendrick made sure I never got my break, and instead of living in a dream, I'm living in a nightmare."

"Well, it didn't always start out that way. Now, it may have turned into a nightmare, but through it all it has brought you back to your dream guy."

I didn't need Kate to feed me a false sense of what this was. This wasn't anything other than me hiring him to do a job. I didn't need any other ideas planted in my head. I didn't need to hear that maybe we would rush back into one another's arms and all would be forgiven. Kendrick would leave me alone and I'd live happily ever after. Life just didn't work that way. At least not for me.

I cleared my throat. "No, Kate, all it means is that

if I choose his company, he will work in my apartment for a few weeks. That's it, that's all."

The waitress dropped off our selection of food, took another drink order from us, and left us to eat. I had just put two pieces of food onto my plate when a sudden flash of light caught my attention. I glanced toward the window in time to see a paparazzi flash a bunch of pictures of Kate and me. Kate turned her attention to the window just in time to see the photographer run off.

"Fuck, they are everywhere!" Kate murmured. "Do you know they tracked me down outside of the drug store the other day. Practically ran me over trying to get a photograph."

"Yeah, it's just because you are famous, unlike me. All those promises and nothing." I shook my head, drinking down the rest of my martini.

"Shut up." Kate laughed. "I assure you all that you have gone through has not been for nothing. You'll get your break. Everything happens for a reason. I say hire Ben. You never know, it may spark some old flames, and if not, at least you get to look at something yummy for a few weeks." She winked.

After lunch, I had gone to the grocery store, and now I carried two heavy brown paper bags full of groceries into the lobby of 425 Las Vegas Boulevard. I had refused help from Jon as I entered the building, even though he said it wasn't a problem. Now I was on my way to the elevator. I hit the button and then struggled with the bags as I stood waiting, wishing that I had taken him up on his offer to help.

Finally, the elevator opened, and I went to step inside when a woman rounded the corner and came running out of the elevator, banging into me.

"Oh my, I am so sorry," a petite brunette said as she straightened herself.

"It's okay," I said, trying to readjust my grip on the bags.

"Did you just move in? I haven't seen you here before." She grinned.

I was just about to answer her when I felt the bag in my left hand start to fall. I did my best to readjust, but it was too late. Not only did that bag fall, but the other bag that was carrying the frozen food had become wet and the bottom fell right out of the bag, spilling the contents all over the floor of the lobby.

"Oh my. Here, let me help you." The brunette scrambled, trying to grab some cans as they rolled away.

I reached into my purse and pulled out two reusable bags that I used to use and handed one to her. She quickly started piling the items into one, while I did the other. Once we had picked everything up, I looked down and saw that I now had three bags to carry instead of two.

"You can't carry all these on your own. Here let me help," she said, hitting the button on the elevator, the doors opening immediately. "What floor are you on?" she asked, picking up two of the bags and stepping into the elevator.

Annoyed with the entire situation, I scooped up the one bag and followed her. "Twenty-fifth."

"Oh, I live on the fifteenth. I'm Carly Lamont."

"Hi, Carly, nice to meet you. I'm Jessica."

Chapter Eleven

Ben

It had been a busy day. I was doing site inspections, making sure all the projects we had running were going smoothly. I also had a conference call with John this afternoon. I'd put him in charge of running the other location, and while I knew he was more than capable, I still needed to be kept up to speed on everything that was going on there.

Armed with a hot coffee, I made my way up the steps to our office. The office was quiet. Julie wasn't behind her desk, so I made my way into my office. I shut the door, flipped on my radio, and pulled my sandwich out of the tiny fridge that sat in the corner. I set everything out on my desk, looking forward to twenty minutes of uninterrupted quiet while I ate.

I had barely bitten into my sandwich when Jules opened the door to my office and leaned against the doorframe, smiling at me.

"What's got you so happy?" I questioned with my mouth full.

"Didn't Dad teach you any manners?"

"What?" I asked, taking another bite. "I'm hungry," I said, talking with my mouth full just to annoy her.

Jules shook her head and laughed. She grabbed the back of the chair and sat down across from me. "So, I got a call from Jessica this morning."

I stopped mid-bite and looked up at my sister who sat there grinning.

"Okay, and?"

"You've got the job. I sent Glenn and his crew over there this morning to start demo."

I glanced at my watch. It was almost three. "You sent them over there this morning? Did you go over all the details or are they just in there ripping shit out randomly?"

"Give me some credit, Ben. I'm not new to this job."

"Yeah, yeah, whatever. That's why you sent the crew over without even following one simple line of instruction."

"What instructions?"

"To let me know if she wants to move ahead with it. I wrote it on the bottom of the quote I left for you," I barked as I jumped up out of my seat, grabbing my sandwich, keys, and paint book.

"Ben, you need to calm down. I tried to call, but your line was busy. Besides, I am following your direction. I'm telling you now aren't I?"

I didn't want to hear it. Ignoring her, I ran out of the office toward the door.

"What about your call with John?" she yelled after me.

"Reschedule," I yelled back.

The crew was already loading their trucks up by the time I pulled up outside of the Las Vegas Boulevard building. I climbed out of my truck and jogged across the street, waving at Glenn.

"Hey, Ben!"

"Hey, man. How did it go today?"

"Great!"

"Please tell me you only ripped out one bathroom?"

"Yeah, Julie already told me, one bathroom at a time. Kitchen last, then paint."

I blew out a breath. "Thank God." Jess had requested that we wouldn't tear apart her entire apartment at once, and I had promised. "Your guys were on their best behavior?"

"Of course," Glenn said, slapping me on the back.

"All right, head on home. See you tomorrow." I looked up at the high-rise and headed back to my truck then started toward the door.

Armed with my binder of paint colors, I knocked on apartment 2501. I felt a funny ping in the pit of my stomach—nerves or excitement at seeing Jess again? I wasn't sure. I was about to knock again when the door opened and Jess stood there smiling at me. "Hey, I didn't think you would make it here today."

"Sorry, I had a few things to take care of, and now that they are finished, I figured I would pop by and we could pick some paint colors."

Jess stood off to the side and opened the door for me to enter. I slipped my shoes off and followed her into the kitchen.

"Want something to drink? I have water, pop, beer..."

"I'll have a beer," I said, watching her as she bent into the fridge and grabbed a bottle for me and water for her. I couldn't help but check out her still-perfect but skinnier ass, my mind going in a direction it really shouldn't. She was just about to turn around when I directed my focus on opening my paint book and pulling out two sample pages.

"Okay, so color. Let's see what you got," she said, smiling as she set the beer bottle down on the counter.

"Okay, so I thought perhaps these colors here would be good for the en suite." I flipped the book over to her so she could look, while I cracked the top off my beer and drank down half the bottle.

Music pounded as I walked into The Dive Bar and spotted Glenn sitting at the bar. I had called him when I left Jess's place to see if he could meet me there. I really needed to unwind.

"Hey, man, I ordered you a beer. Should be here any second," Glenn said as I took a seat next to him.

"Thanks. I sure as hell need it right now."

"What's going on? I haven't seen you so worked up over a job as you were this afternoon. Even Julie mentioned something to me as I walked into the office tonight."

Glenn was one of my very first hires for this part of the company, and I couldn't be more grateful for him. We had worked so closely together over the last five years that we had formed a quick and solid friendship. He and his wife treated me like I was part of their family and for that I was grateful.

"Fucking Jules. She needs to learn how to keep her mouth shut," I mumbled.

"Ben, what the hell is going on? You're never like this."

I shrugged and took a drink of the ice cold beer that had been placed down in front of me. I didn't want to talk about work or Jules or Jess. I just wanted to unwind with a close friend.

"It's nothing, man. Guess stress is just getting me."

"That's why you should have taken that vacation. I could have handled everything you needed."

Glenn should have talked to Jules, who apparently didn't see that. I shrugged. "I know, but it's not my style, you know."

"I know."

"So this job at Las Vegas Boulevard, you seem possessive over it. Jules told me you would be stopping by today. Is there anything I need to know?"

I scratched at the label on my bottle. "Nope, you know all you need to know about that. It's just a quick job is all."

Glenn looked at me with suspicion. "Ben, you've given us two weeks to get the entire job done. A job that normally would take a minimum of six to eight weeks. I'm surprised you could get everything ordered in time."

"I pulled a few strings. She wanted a quick turnaround. Besides it's a lot of money to the company, so what was I supposed to do?"

Glenn grabbed a handful of nuts from the dish in the center of the table and washed them down with his beer. "Normally, you would tell the person it takes time. I mean you pulled my crew off another job to get this one done. I also know that you took the countertops that were ordered for the Wiggins build and are using those. That will end up meaning my guys will have to work double time on the other job to get that one completed, not to mention you'll have to replace the countertops. Please don't think I'm complaining, but—"

"Good, then stop complaining. It's just important and needs to get done, that's it. As for the other job, it's my problem. I will deal with the clients. Hell, I'll do the work myself if I have to, to keep everything on time."

Glenn shrugged and turned his attention to the hockey game that was on the screen over the bar. I wanted to tell Glenn all about Jess, all about what had happened, and all about how I was feeling. Instead, I was my normal grumpy self for the rest of the night. I mean what guy goes on and on whining about the woman who got away.

Chapter Twelve

JESSICA

I was meeting Kate at Mad House for our usual coffee date. It was Wednesday morning, and we had agreed that we wouldn't let our new location mess our tradition up. I approached the building, swung my purse over my shoulder, and walked over to the table where she sat.

"Morning, pumpkin," she sang as she closed her favorite weekly gossip mag, *Everyday Celebrity*, and smiled.

"I can't believe you can get that rag all the way out here." I laughed, sitting down across from her, reaching for the filth she was reading, but she stopped me by reaching out and gripping the magazine. I smiled, tugging harder, but she ripped the magazine from my hand and shoved it into her purse.

"No, you don't! I didn't come to meet you to watch you read that garbage. Now why don't you tell me all about this handsome contractor. Did you hire him? Was he there yesterday walking around shirtless?" she said with a smile. "You know, I think I may come by for a coffee later."

I frowned. "Kate, why are you acting weird?" I said, looking at her. "What are you hiding? Why won't you let me flip through that magazine while we have coffee?"

"Because I want to hear all about Ben," she said, flashing her fake smile, still shoving the magazine deeper into her purse.

"You don't want to hear about Ben, and I know you won't come, and I know you, you won't scope him out." I smiled. "Plus, I've seen that smile on your face before. You're hiding something, spill it," I said, nodding toward her bag. "What was in that magazine?"

Kate pulled her hand from inside the bag and placed her hands under her chin, trying to look innocent just in time for her cell phone to ring. I watched as her eyes flashed to the screen, a look of horror in them. She immediately shut the screen off, ignoring the ringing phone, and then she looked back to me, trying to hide the look of discomfort.

"Aren't you going to answer that?" I nodded at the ringing phone. "It could be important."

"No, it's nothing important. Probably just a solicitor, and you know how I hate those calls."

"I do, but it could also be your agent. Aren't you waiting on news of a shoot?"

"Nope, no, I already received that call. I can assure you it's nothing. Now spill it," she said, looking at her ringing phone and swallowing hard.

I frowned and was just about to interrogate her when out of the corner of my eye I saw the girl who helped me with my groceries. She waved the second she spotted us and approached our table. "I knew I knew you. I was second-guessing myself, but you are her," she said, holding up the same magazine Kate had tried so hard to hide, looking at me then back to the page.

"I'm who? What are you talking about?" I asked. I wasn't used to being recognized anymore. It had been a few years since I'd last been in an ad, and once you're out of the limelight, you just start blending in with everyone else. Now the only time I was recognized was when I was on Kendrick's arm, which wasn't often.

"The other day after I helped you with your groceries, I was talking to my boyfriend, John. I said you looked like Jessica Hayward. I used to follow you when you first started. I always thought you were prettier than half of the models out there, but then you just fizzled out. John assured me there was no way that it was you, but here it is in black and white," she said, throwing the tabloid down on the table to show me the picture of Kate and me from the restaurant the other night.

I scanned the image and then looked to the print under the image, *'Jessica Hayward & Kate Green'*, then I looked to the headline. *'Trouble in Paradise, could it be true: Kendrick and Jessica, Over?'*

The contents of my stomach threatened to rise as I began to read the article. Kendrick always read this piece of shit rag to make sure his name wasn't in it. He always said it was the worst place he could ever be, that it would be a career killer for him. If he saw this, which I was sure he would, he would know where I was.

Kate's phone rang again, and once again she shut the screen off to hide whoever was calling. I tore my eyes from the article and glanced over at her. She shook her head at me. I knew immediately that it was Kendrick. "Just answer it," I mumbled. "I already know it's Kendrick."

I glanced back over at Carly, who still stood at the edge of the table. "I was wondering, would I be able to get your autograph?" she asked, holding out a pen for me to sign. I had no clue why she was still standing here bothering me. Kate was way more famous than me. Regardless, I took her pen and scribbled my signature below my picture.

"Thank you so much. Have a marvelous day! I'll see you around. We will be the best of friends, I just know it," she said, taking the magazine and heading out the door.

I turned to Kate. "How many times has he called you?" I asked, no longer interested in the cup of coffee that sat in front of me.

"He's been calling upwards of ten times a day since Monday. His messages are getting more and more violent."

"When did this article come out?" I questioned as my stomach turned. Kate handed me the magazine, and I checked the date on the front. It had come out Monday, a few days after the picture had been taken. I was about to say something when Kate's phone rang out again. "Just answer the phone, Kate."

She looked at me. "Are you sure?"

I nodded. One more ring and she picked up the phone. "Hello, Kate Green," she said, doing her best to disguise her voice with a calm and cool demeanor.

"Kate, it's Kendrick," I heard his raised voice bark over the phone.

"Good morning, Kendrick. How are you?" Kate's

eyes met mine, and I could tell she was trying her best to be friendly.

"Have you seen Jessica?"

I sat there shaking my head, begging her not to tell him I was sitting here with her.

"Make something up," I mouthed, praying that perhaps he hadn't seen the magazine and that he was legitimately worried about me.

"No, I'm in Vegas, Kendrick, doing a spread for a magazine. I'd assume she was at home."

The line went quiet for a second. Then I heard him clear his throat. "You don't have any idea where she might be?"

I could hear Kendrick's voice on the other end of the phone as he asked her the question and could already hear the irritation and annoyance in his voice.

"Goodness no. I've been here for the last couple of weeks. Come to think of it, I haven't even spoken to her. Is everything all right? Did you try calling the apartment."

Kate was doing her best to cover for me, that much was apparent, but Kendrick was smart. If he had seen the article, I knew that if he wasn't already here, he would be on the next plane in a matter of minutes.

"Don't lie to me. Where do you think I am? Besides, I saw the picture in *The Morning Observer* and in

Everyday Celebrity. I know she is with you. After all, it is ten in the morning on a Wednesday. I know she doesn't think I know that you both meet up every Wednesday, but I do. That petty bitch will ruin my career!"

Kate shook her head at me and mouthed the words "he knows" at me. Kate put the phone onto speaker and lay the phone in the middle of the table so I could hear the rest of the conversation.

"Why don't you tell Jessica to look out the window over her left shoulder," Kendrick bit out.

I looked up at Kate, meeting her eyes, and then we both turned and looked out the window at the same time. Immediately, I spotted the same man with the camera across the street, the flash going off instantly.

Immediately, Kate ended the call with Kendrick and looked at me. "Not only was the article in *Everyday Celebrity*, but they also printed it in *The Morning Observer*."

I felt sick to my stomach. "I've got to go," I said, reaching for my jacket and bag. "He probably sent that guy here."

"What? No way. He's just being a bully. Come on, Jess," Kate cried.

"No, no, he isn't. I can guarantee you he is coming here. He probably flew home the second he saw the articles. I know him. Besides, I can't be late. Ben is on his way to the apartment. I am supposed to approve of the final paint colors so he can grab what he needs." I kissed her on the cheek.

"At least let me drive you home," Kate said, throwing a fifty dollar bill down in the middle of the table before grabbing her stuff and running after me.

I'd been home for twenty minutes. I stood in the bathroom, looking in the mirror at my tear-stained cheeks. I ran a cloth under the warm water and wiped my face. I thought I had gotten away with running away and leaving that hellish life with Kendrick behind. I'd hoped that I would have just faded into the enormous sea of people and that he would never find me. I had been so wrong and should have known better. He would always find me, just as he had promised so many times when I would threaten of leaving before. Perhaps I should have spoken to Hunter Malone about a restraining order or and divorce as well so I could have started proceedings while Kendrick had been gone. That way the documents would have been waiting for him upon his arrival back home. Only now it was too late.

A sharp knock on the door caused me to jump. I glanced at my reflection in the mirror. My eyes were still red and puffy, which would definitely give it away that I'd been crying. I dabbed my eyes with the now cold cloth I held in my hand, gave my face a final wipe, and threw the cloth on the edge of the sink.

I opened the door and came face-to-face with a stack of tiles being held by a pair of hands.

"Just me." Ben chuckled.

I stepped off to the side, trying to hide my face while Ben brought in the tile samples. I shut the door behind him and took a deep breath before I turned around. Ben had always been observant, and I knew he would notice instantly. I hadn't even made eye contact when I turned around and his deep voice floated through the apartment. "Jess, are you all right?"

I didn't answer him immediately. My eyes floated to the lot of tile samples that he'd placed on the couch. "I love the color choices you picked. Honestly, they couldn't be more perfect." I smiled, fighting the lump in my throat. I didn't have to say anything. He already knew something was wrong, and the instant we made eye contact I crumbled. Burying my face in my hands, I turned away from Ben and began to cry.

It was a matter of seconds before I felt his familiar,

long-lost touch. His strong hands softly but firmly gripping my shoulders were as soothing as they'd been all those years ago. He slowly turned me and pulled me against him. I didn't fight him. Instead, I rested my head against his chest and wrapped my arms around his waist. His natural scent invaded my nose, comforting me, just like it used to do when we were younger. He said nothing. We just stood like that for a while, his arms around me, his chin on top of my head, until the tears finally stopped.

"Care to tell me what is going on?" he asked as I stepped away.

I blew out a breath and wiped the remains of my tears from my cheeks. "Got ten years?" I laughed.

"You're in luck because I've got all the time you need," he said, going to the fridge and pulling out two beers. He cracked the tops and held a bottle out for me to take.

"Oh, I um, don't drink beer anymore," I said, shaking my head. It was a habit I had fallen into, the words rolling off my tongue just as they had trained me to do, like they belonged there.

"Everything is easier to talk about with a beer," he said, taking a swig. "Drink up."

I reached and took the bottle, and just like when we were teens, I brought it to my lips, letting the cold, refreshing liquid roll down my throat. It had been so long since I'd had one that I almost forgot what it tasted like.

"So why don't you drink beer anymore?" he questioned.

"Beer bloats. Plus, Kendrick doesn't like it when I drink anything, never mind beer. He says it does nothing but add on extra calories that I don't need."

"Kendrick?"

"Kendrick is my husband. I met him shortly after I left home and went to LA. He's an agent. He was looking for a young model. He promised me he could get me connected to the big-time agencies. He promised me that he knew people. I went to parties with him, eventually ended up dating him. Unfortunately for me, I didn't know any better. He introduced me to people, but not the right people. I got handed a few jobs, but it was only a matter of time before I began questioning everything. Before him I had been doing better on my own, but he convinced me that the types of contracts I wanted take time. So, I trusted him, then we got engaged, and then married, and six years later, here I am. There's still no big contracts or any of the magic people he had promised, and as for my career, it has completely fizzled."

Ben looked at me. I was expecting to see an I told you so look, but I didn't see that. Instead, I saw pity. "I see."

I glanced at Ben. I could see it in his eyes. He knew what was really going on. He had never been a stupid man. "When I got news of my grandfather dying, I mentioned nothing to Kendrick. I was planning on leaving him anyway, so I ran with my friend Kate."

"Why were you planning on leaving him? I mean, aside from the issue with your career, it looks like he has taken care of you. You have nice clothes, you look good, a little thin for my liking, but overall you don't look like you are lacking for anything."

"No, you're right, I am not lacking in that regard. He has provided a suitable home for me, but it's the rest of it."

"What do you mean by the rest of it?" he questioned.

I knew he was waiting for me to say the words. Instead, I took another mouthful of beer and picked at the label on the bottle.

"What is the rest of it, Jess?"

"He's been cheating on me with other models—you know, the younger ones. We have...a very broken marriage that I am running away from, and..." I stopped. I couldn't utter the words, the truth of him hitting me.

"What else is there, Jess?"

I didn't want to admit it, but the words just flowed from my mouth. "He's controlling and abusive. He controls every penny I spend, every calorie I eat, and I had been here about a week before I could let anyone in this apartment because of..." I stopped and turned away so Ben couldn't see my face. I walked over to the window and looked down at the bustling city below, wishing that this wasn't happening to me.

"Because of what, Jess?"

"The bruises on my face."

Ben was quiet for a moment, and I turned to look at him. "Well, at least he doesn't know where you are, so that is a good thing."

"That's not true. Apparently, paparazzi were following Kate and got a picture of us in a restaurant. Once the magazine got the image, they saw me and turned the article into some sort of divorce inquiry. Kendrick saw it, and now he knows where I am. He called Kate today. He's coming to get me, and he is pissed." I glanced at Ben, who now gripped the beer bottle in his hand so hard his knuckles were white. "Say something... please," I begged.

It was like someone had turned on a switch. He loosened his grip on the bottle, finally putting it down on the counter, and walked over to the couch, picking up the tiles. He brought them over and set them on the counter, reaching down and picking up the sample of the cupboard door, laying everything side by side. "Do you like these?"

I frowned. Was he not going to say anything in response to what I had told him? Did he not care that my life was in danger and that it would only be a matter of days, maybe even hours before Kendrick found me?

"Ben?"

"What do you think, seeing them all together like this? It's much easier to envision the completed kitchen. If you don't like them, I have more samples down in my truck. I can go get those," he said, staring at everything that lay on the counter.

"Ben? Aren't you going to say anything?"

Ben let out a breath and placed his arms on the counter in front of him, his forearms and biceps flexing. "Jess, I said something once, long ago, that I shouldn't have said. My words took you away from me, and I learned an important lesson from it. So, I'm not about to interfere again. This isn't my problem to solve. So, as much as I hate the fact that he has put his hands on you, and that he treats you the way you say he does, it's not my place to get involved again. I'm here for a renovation, nothing more."

"Seriously?" I was dumbfounded. He wasn't even going to help me.

"Yes." He looked like he wanted to say something else, but stopped before he could say the words.

"What? What were you going to say?" I glared at

him as he kept his face down on the tile samples in front of him.

"I will not do or say anything because watching you walk away from me the first time was the hardest thing I've ever had to deal with. It was harder on me than having to bury my father." Once those words had passed his lips, he picked up the tile samples, stacking them together. "I've got to go," he mumbled, slipping his shoes on.

I stood there in a state of shock as the door slammed shut. Kendrick could be in the city any moment, and now Ben knew my secret. My body was in overdrive with all that I'd learned today. Hearing the truth from Ben that I had been harder to get over than the loss of his own father had thrown me. I'd figured Ben had long forgotten about me.

Chapter Thirteen

Ben

Opening the fridge door, I stood staring at a bunch of empty shelves debating on what to have for dinner. I pulled out a jar of dill pickles, the only thing in my fridge, and opened it to find mold covering the lid. I apparently needed to do a grocery run. Dumping the juice off the pickles, I put the lid back on the jar and dumped it into the garbage can.

My mind hadn't shut off since I left Jess's place over two hours ago. I needed to get it through my head that she wasn't nor would she become my problem. She had thrown me away a long time ago, and for her now to turn to me for help wasn't fair.

I looked back in the fridge at the empty shelves as if food would magically appear and then slammed the fridge door shut, still hearing her words "he's controlling and abusive." They rang through my mind loud and clear. I balled my fists. It didn't matter if she wasn't my problem. I could look the other way on the cheating part, but I detested men who laid their hands on women. Just ask my sister.

I went back to the fridge and pulled out the only thing edible in my apartment: a cold beer. I twisted the cap off, took a long swig, letting the cool liquid slide down my throat, and flopped down on the couch. Reaching for the remote, I turned on the hockey game and did my best to get lost in anything other than Jess's issues.

A harsh knock on the back door caused me to jump and drop the remote on the floor. I glanced at the clock. It was almost eight; the three beers I'd had had quelled the hunger pangs. I looked around my messy living room and yelled, "Come in," from where I lay, sure that it was probably Glenn or one of the other guys from work.

I heard the door squeak open, reminding me of something else that should be added to the already extensive list of things I had to fix. I made a mental note to get that taken care of over the weekend, when the smell of pizza hit my nose, and my stomach let out a loud groan.

"Hey, just me," Julie yelled. "Did you forget? You were supposed to meet me tonight at The Dive Bar?"

Instantly, I remembered and I closed my eyes. "Fuck! Sorry, Jules. I got a little sidetracked," I said, forcing myself up off the couch and heading to the kitchen to meet my sister.

"It's fine. I brought pizza and wings to you instead. I figured you got caught up in something, but it would have been nice for you to call me or something. Instead, I sat there waiting for you for an hour, looking like an idiot."

It had totally slipped my mind that my sister and I had dinner plans. I walked over to the counter and flipped open the pizza box, grabbing a slice, while my sister grabbed plates from the cupboard. Her eyes fell to the stack of dirty dishes that lined the counters, and then she turned and looked me over, watching as a piece of pepperoni fell onto my chest, which I grabbed and shoved in my mouth.

"Jesus, you look like shit! Here, have a plate." She giggled and thrust the plate out to me. "You probably should clean this place up, you know. It's a sty. Honestly, for a guy who is looking for a girlfriend, you'd think you'd keep your place clean."

"Thanks! Always loved your compliments. Since when did you become my keeper anyway?"

Jules completely ignored me while I loaded my

plate with pizza and wings. While she loaded hers, I grabbed two beers from the fridge, pulled the chair out, and sat down at the table. I twisted off the two caps and handed her a bottle.

"So what happened?" she asked, taking the beer from my hand.

"Apparently, I'm a shitty-looking guy who lives in a sty. What do you mean, what happened?"

"You stood me up, for starters, but in all seriousness, you look like you've been put through the mill. I know your day wasn't that tough, since I'm the one who scheduled it, so what gives?"

The last thing I wanted to do was talk about Jess, but I knew it was inevitable with my sister. She would poke, prod, and pry until I had spilled everything! The fact that she hadn't asked me more than she already had surprised me, especially since she knew I had gone to Jess's earlier.

"Something happen between you and Jess?"

There it was, like always. I threw my slice of pizza down on the plate and brought the beer bottle up to my lips. "Guess you could say that." I guzzled down half the bottle and looked at my sister.

"Care to elaborate or are you going to make love to that beer bottle all night?" she asked while picking a piece of pepperoni off her pizza and shoving it into her mouth.

"Remember Rod?"

"As in my Rod?" she questioned, frowning at me for bringing him up.

"Yeah."

"You remember what he used to do to you?"

Julie went quiet. Her relationship with Rod wasn't one we talked about much, if ever, after what had happened. Rod was a cheater. Jules had confronted him on the fact that she had seen him out with another woman, and that night she had called me in a panic to come and get her. I had rushed to her place, but I was too late. I had found her face down in a pool of her own blood with a broken nose and fractured jaw. I got her to safety, and then I had gone back and waited for him to return home. Once he did, I beat him within an inch of his life.

"It's not something I could easily forget," she mumbled. "Why are you bringing him up?" Her eyes grew wide. "Oh God, he wasn't there, was he?"

"No, he wasn't there, but I think him and Jess's husband could be related." I chuckled. "Jess admitted to me today that her husband, or ex-husband, or whoever the fuck he is, abuses her. I swear, Jules, I saw red. I wanted to tear the guy limb from limb. Every inch of my body was on fire."

"Ben, it's not your place," Julie warned. "She isn't your problem anymore."

"I know, but seriously, Jules..."

"Seriously what? You want to take a swing at him? Finish him off like you did Rod. I shouldn't have to remind you that it was all we could do to keep you out of jail after what you did to Rod. I can't do it again. You can't do it again. She isn't yours to protect. She's a distant memory, at best."

I thought hard about what Jules was saying. The ache in my gut said differently. "All right, so then what do I do?"

"You walk away. You continue down your path and let her continue down hers. I can also tell you what not to do. Don't let her push her hard-luck story on you. Don't fall pray to her. She made her decision a long time ago. That decision didn't involve you then, and it shouldn't involve you now."

"If she didn't want me to tell her what to do, then why did she bother telling me at all?"

"Ben, I can't answer for her. All I can do is speculate that perhaps she is lonely, she's probably scared. Whatever you do, just stay out of it. It's her problem."

"Let me ask you, why did you tell me about Rod?"

"You're my brother. Besides, I was different. I wanted the help, and even though I had told you, I was almost too late. Ben, I was face down in a pool of my blood. He would have eventually killed me if I stayed, if he didn't kill me that night."

I drank down the rest of my beer and looked at my sister. "Jules, what am I supposed to do?"

"The only thing you should do is finish the job, that's it. I don't even know why you feel compelled to do more, but if you must do more than that, just support her and be her friend. Be there to listen when she needs it. Just don't get involved in the middle of a situation you know nothing of, and certainly don't get involved with her again. She hurt you so badly. You need to meet a nice girl. One who will be happy with the life you can provide."

I sat back against the chair and threw the slice of pizza I was about to sink my teeth into back onto the plate. "Why would you think I would try to get her back?"

Jules looked dumbfounded. "Really, Ben? You have to ask? You're still carrying around a ring you gave her years ago. I don't really know why that thought would even cross my mind," she said, rolling her eyes at me.

"So what? So I carry around a memento!"

"No." She laughed to herself. "No, Ben, I know you. It's not a memento. It's something that represents her. Honestly, I think the fact of the matter is you have never let her go. I think you have held onto a dream of her coming back and wanting another chance. I think that is why you feel compelled to do something about her situation. You think that if you save her she will come back to you. What you really need to do is just let her go. I don't want to see you get hurt again. So just please take my advice, like I took yours when I didn't want to trust anyone."

Jules was right, I had never let Jess go, and now was not the time to try to get her back, no matter how badly I may have thought I might want another chance with her. I'd been down that road before. I nodded, picking up my slice of pizza and biting off a mouthful. "Thanks for the talk, Jules," I said, raising my beer bottle to hers and clinking them together.

We ate the rest of our dinner in silence and then watched the rest of the hockey game. Before Jules left, she gave me a hand cleaning up the kitchen, and then she was on her way out my door, leaving me to fight my own demons for the night.

I stood in the hallway on the other side of the door to apartment 2501. I could hear her voice through the door, and then another female voice, then two women laughed. It sounded good to hear Jess laugh like that. I held onto the coffees I had brought and knocked gently on the door. It was early for most people, only nine, and I was showing up unannounced, but I figured perhaps Jess would like to go with me to order the granite for the countertops and the tile this morning.

The door was abruptly pulled open, and I watched as first shock and then a slight smile spread across her face. "Good morning," she said hesitantly. "I didn't forget about an appointment with you, did I?"

I glanced inside and saw a petite brunette sitting on the couch. "No, I just thought you might like to join me to pick the tiles and granite for the countertops. If you are busy, I can go and get it done."

Jess glanced over her shoulder at the brunette who nodded and stood. "Guess that is my cue," she said, giggling.

Jess turned back to me. "Sure, that sounds like it would be fun." Jess stepped to the side, inviting me in.

"This is my friend, Carly. She lives a few floors down."

"Hi, Carly, I'm Ben."

"Hi, Ben. Geez, you're a sexy thing," she said, winking at me. "Well, Jess, I will see you later okay. Have fun."

I watched as Carly leaned in and whispered

something to Jess, causing her face to flush. Jess hugged her, and once she had left, she shut the door behind her.

Twenty minutes later, we were walking through the wholesale shop looking at slabs of granite. "What do you think of this one? It's light enough but still compliments."

I watched as Jess ran her hand over the smooth piece of granite, smiling. "I think it would be perfect."

"All right then, you're sure? You can only choose once you know," I said, winking at her. "I remember how indecisive you always were."

"Yeah, I'm sure. I think you're right. It fits perfectly."

"All right, so just to recap..." I said, pulling out all the tile selections she had made, laying them on top of the piece for the counter. "Does it all look okay?"

"Yes."

"All right, the order is going in then." I stepped off to the side and began placing the order with the sales rep. I kept watching Jess as she stood looking over everything. A funny smile came over her face, followed by an immediate look of sadness. I signed the order form and handed it to the guy behind the counter to process and then joined Jess again.

"What's on that mind of yours?" I questioned.

She huffed. "Just memories. Memories of our plans

when we were younger to remodel homes together. Sometimes, I wish I'd taken that path instead of the one I did." She lifted her eyes to mine.

"Well, we are remodeling a place together, silly." My finger taping her chin.

"I guess." She smiled softly. "Did you want to come back to my place for dinner?"

I glanced at my watch, the words of my sister running through my mind not to get involved. I knew she was right on so many levels, but on so many levels my gut was telling me just to go for it.

"If there is somewhere you need to be just say so," she mumbled when I didn't answer right away.

"Nope, I'm all yours. Just trying to decide what to grab for dinner," I said, smiling.

"Oh." She smiled again, this time turning away from me.

Three hours later, we lay sprawled out on a blanket in her living room. We both lay on our sides, our heads resting on our hands as we shared a bowl of popcorn. Once the bowl was empty, I pulled it out from between us and reached back to set it on the coffee table. I turned back to find Jess on her back, staring up at the ceiling, a faraway look on her face.

"You remember that old house, the one we used to make out at? "

"The one I fixed up with my dad?" I questioned,

my mind instantly transporting me to the spot we used to frequent.

"Yeah, that's the one."

"What about it?" I asked, studying her face.

"What ever happened to it?"

"Well, we finished it that summer. Dad already had a buyer, so I'm guessing they must have moved in."

"Did it turn out as well as we had thought it would?"

"Yeah, it was okay I guess." I didn't have the heart to tell her I had basically been a robot the rest of that summer, that I barely remembered anything after she had immediately left. That the memories of that place had been buried so deep in my subconscious that I never thought about it.

She grew quiet, staring up at the ceiling, lost in thought. I just lay beside her and watched her. I could tell she wanted to ask me something, and I was about to ask her when she looked into my eyes. "Did you ever think of us? After I left, I mean."

I ran my hand over my face. This wasn't a conversation I wanted or needed to be having right now. She didn't know the half of it. Instead of answering her, I simply nodded.

"Did you ever wonder what would have happened had I not left?" she questioned, rolling over and propping herself up and looking at me.

"Did you?" I asked, looking into her eyes.

"All the time," she whispered, turning her eyes away from mine.

Something about the look in her eyes when she turned them down to the floor had me wishing that she would look at me again. It was as if someone else took over my body, and in slow motion I leaned forward, placing my hand under her chin. I tapped her chin with my fingers, encouraging her to look up. The instant our eye met, I leaned forward and met her lips. Slowly and gently at first, my lips grazed over hers, barely even touching them. Then, with a little more intensity, my lips pressed against hers and I kissed her again. When we parted, the only words on my lips were a mumbled, "I never once stopped thinking of you."

Chapter Fourteen

The first thought on my mind when I woke this morning was the kiss that Ben and I had shared last night. I felt lighter than I had in years and was excited to get this remodel finished. I had a ton of ideas for how to decorate the place to make sure it would sell. I spent the morning boxing up some of my grandfather's things. I had rented a storage unit, and once the place sold, I would take my time going through everything, deciding what I wanted to keep and what I wanted to get rid of.

I had taken a break and stood in the kitchen eating a piece of toast while dialing Kate's number. I was hoping she would be up for some shopping today, but she told me she was busy this morning. I thought about calling Ben to see if he wanted to accompany me, but I didn't want to appear needy or pushy. Plus, I was sure he was working all day.

Armed with a travel mug full of coffee, I ventured out and now stood sifting through items at the home decor store. In an hour, my cart was overflowing with candleholders, centerpieces, and a ton of other things that were probably nothing but money wasters.

I turned the cart and headed into the pillow section. Tons of accent pillows lined the walls. I picked neutral colors, throwing four on top of my insanely packed buggy. When I was content that I had everything, I began wandering through the aisles to the front of the store where a box of wine glasses caught my eye. They weren't something I needed, but something I wanted, and I reached for them, picking up the box and reading the funny sayings on them.

I was about to throw them into the cart when someone gripped my elbow harshly, causing me to jump and drop the box. The second the box hit the floor, the glasses shattered, drawing attention to myself.

"Well, well..." was all I heard. The familiar deep voice whispered in my ear, "Don't make a scene,

Jessica." Kendrick's voice drawled as he tightened his grip on my elbow, "Just come with me, easy as that."

I was tempted to fight him, tempted to scream, but instead I froze. Surely, someone in this store would see what was going on and would help me, I thought. I was about to say something to Kendrick when he tightened his grip on my arm, causing me pain. Instead of my original plan, I ripped my purse from the seat of the buggy and walked away from the cart, leaving the mess of broken glass all over the floor.

I heard women murmur as I walked through the store with Kendrick close behind, still gripping my arm. They all looked my way, but none of them said or did anything.

Kendrick finally loosened his hold on me, and I took a of couple steps in front of him, hoping to get away. Kendrick had already noticed, and he reached out gripping my bicep once again, pulling me back toward him. People continued to stare at us as he marched me through the store like I was some five-year-old child who had done something wrong.

The second we were outside, he shoved me in the direction of his car, his fingers digging harder into my arm. "Fuck, Kendrick, you are hurting me," I tried stating forcefully. "Let go of me."

"You've humiliated me!" he barked, shoving me

against the side of his car while he pulled the door open.

"You've humiliated yourself!" I spat. "If people really knew what you were like, you would have nothing. Hitting on young, innocent women and screwing them over. Just like you did to me when I was younger. You probably ruined my career on purpose. No one else is to blame."

"Get in the car," he gritted through his teeth, his body invading my space as he stepped in closer, looking down into my face.

I glared at him, preparing for a fight, but then I saw the flash of anger in his eyes, and I knew I didn't stand a chance against him. His six-foot-two frame stood over me, and he outweighed me by a hundred and twenty pounds. He would finish me.

Instead of creating any more of a scene than we already had, I complied and crawled into the front seat. He slammed the door, running around to the driver's side and getting in.

"So," he barked as he fired the engine, "I had to find out the hard way that my wife left me, huh? You stupid bitch," Kendrick said, flicking my wedding ring at me. "Leaving it in a dish on a table. Either you were praying I wouldn't see it, or secretly you wanted me to find it. Which was it?"

"It shouldn't come as a shock to you, Kendrick.

You are always off with other women. I shouldn't be treated that way, and frankly, I don't want your ring anymore, so I gave it back to you."

"Ha, you gave it back? That ring you tossed cost me 1.2 million dollars. Surely, you could use the money. Where are you staying anyway? The article said you were spotted outside of 425 Las Vegas Boulevard, isn't that right?" he said, driving in the building's direction.

I said nothing. I crossed my arms over my chest and sat there tight-lipped.

"You humiliated me in front of everyone. My career has gone down the drain, thanks to that little article. Do you know that when clients started seeing the news that we could be over, they wanted to leave!" he yelled, swerving to miss a car.

"What is it, Kendrick? Are you afraid that they see you for who you really are? A nasty, nasty man, a liar and a cheat," I screamed as his tires screeched to avoid hitting someone.

"You bitch! You are coming back with me. You will pay for everything you have caused me to lose." He pulled into a parking spot on the side of the street and jammed on the brakes. He wasted no time getting out of the car and running around to my side.

He opened the door and reached in, pulling me out roughly. "Where are we going?" I screamed.

"You are getting your things, and we are going back to LA. No questions, and don't make a scene. You're not calling Kate. You're not mentioning anything to anybody. Just do as you're fucking told. Go up to her place, get your shit, and get your ass back down here."

He squeezed my arms tight, pushing me away from the car, and slapped me across the face. As I turned my head to look at Kendrick, the same paparazzi that had followed Kate and I stood at the end of Kendrick's car, camera pointed. He snapped away pictures. "Ah, this will be so good," he muttered as he continued to click away while Kendrick held onto me.

Kendrick shoved me to the ground for a chance to grab the paparazzi's camera. The paparazzi took off, and Kendrick grabbed me, picking me up. The second I was on my feet, I lifted my knee and kicked Kendrick in the balls, a whoosh of air escaping his lips as he doubled over in pain. I took that as my chance, and without thinking, I ran right into traffic, dodging cars with their horns blaring, tires squealing as they hit their brakes to avoid hitting me.

I was almost across the road when I glanced behind me and saw Kendrick lunge into traffic. He'd forgotten all about the paparazzi who stood across the street taking pictures as he ran toward me, dodging cars. I continued running, finally making it to the sidewalk, when I heard a squeal of tires on the pavement. I turned around and watched breathlessly as a red truck plowed into Kendrick, sending him flying into the air. Immediately, my hands covered my mouth to keep from screaming as I watched Kendrick fall into another car, bouncing off that and landing on the pavement. I blinked hard and took a look. Kendrick lay on the pavement in a very unnatural position.

Cars came screeching to a halt, drivers getting out and looking to the man who lay in a heap in the center of the road. "Someone call 911," I heard someone say.

I could barely move, and then I looked at the red truck. That was when the door opened and I watched Carly climb out of the driver's side. She stared down at Kendrick's body and then up to me, horror in her eyes. I felt as if I had no control over my body as I slowly walked over to her. Once at her side, she looked up at me. "Are you okay?"

I nodded, looking back over my shoulder where Kendrick lay in a heap on the pavement. "I think so," I murmured.

"I saw you jut out into traffic. He was after you. I didn't mean to hit him. He just kind of ran in front of me."

"He was after me, Carly," I said, turning my head

so she could see the fresh slap that he had delivered only moments before.

Sirens started wailing in the background as police and an ambulance arrived on the scene. It was only a matter of moments before the paramedics had taken Kendrick, with zero vital signs, to the hospital, and we were being questioned by the police.

Chapter Fifteen

Ben

I was sure my heart had stopped when Jess had called from the Las Vegas Police Department to tell me that there had been an accident. I had rushed down to the department to find Jess crying in the hallway. I had finally calmed her down just in time for us to receive the news that Kendrick had succumbed to his injuries. Jess had only nodded as she received the news. She made no comment. She just gripped my hand tightly while she listened.

Once Carly was released from questioning, I drove them both back to the apartment. I was afraid that at any point during the drive, Jess would break down, but instead she was quiet as we entered the elevator.

We walked Carly up to her place, where the girls

hugged for a few moments before saying good night. Then I rode the elevator up to her floor, her hand in mine. I took the key from Jess and pushed the door to her apartment open, turned on the light, and let her walk in before me, my hand resting on her lower back. "Why don't you take a seat on the couch and relax. I'll make you some tea."

Jess nodded. "I think I will take a shower and get changed."

Those had been the only words Jess had muttered since she had called me to come and pick her up. I watched as she slipped her shoes off and wandered down the hall to her bedroom. She shut the door behind her, while I went into the half-torn-apart kitchen, filled the kettle, and put it on to boil. She'd been in the shower for almost half an hour, and while waiting for her, I pulled the blinds and turned on the TV, letting the noise drown out the silence. I'd just gone into the kitchen when I saw her out of the corner of my eye.

"Are you hungry?" Jess asked, coming around the corner. She was dressed in sweats, and she lay down and curled into a ball in the middle of the couch.

"I could eat," I said, glancing at my watch, realizing I hadn't eaten since breakfast. "Feel like Chinese?"

I watched as her eyes lit up at the idea. "My

goodness, do I ever. It's been years since I had Chinese."

"All right, give me a minute." I chuckled as I did an internet search for the nearest Chinese restaurant and picked up the phone. I placed a rather large order from China Garden, so Jess could have leftovers. "Should be here shortly," I said and put the phone back on the charger. "I ordered enough so you can have it tomorrow night too."

"Perfect. I'm so hungry."

The kettle whistled, and I quickly stopped and poured the boiling water over a tea bag. "Here you go," I said, setting the cup down on the table in front of Jess. "You okay?" I questioned, sitting down beside her.

She sat there staring into the cup of tea I had just brought to her. "I just can't believe he's gone. It feels kind of surreal, you know? I'm free. I can do whatever I want. I can eat what I want, go where I want, without having to answer to him."

"You are, and now he definitely can't hurt you anymore," I replied, taking in the bruise I'd noticed earlier that had been forming on her cheek. "Does this hurt?" I asked, reaching out and cupping her cheek, running my thumb gently over the puffy green-and-yellow bruise, causing her to flinch.

"A little," she whispered. "Really, though, it's nothing. They've been much worse."

I frowned. Nothing. What did she mean nothing? In my mind, Kendrick was lucky he was dead. I got up from the couch and went to the kitchen. I placed a few ice cubes in a bag and wrapped it in a towel. "Here, keep this on it. It should help with the swelling." I held the wrap up to her cheek.

Her fingers grazed mine as she took the ice from me and held it against her cheek. I sat down beside her as she rested her head in my lap. I pulled her hair back off her face and soon found my fingers running through her soft hair, just as I used to do when we were younger. She gave a soft little moan and closed her eyes.

We'd stayed that way for close to half an hour. The longer I sat there staring down at her, the longer I thought about how badly I wanted to kiss her again. The urge built, and soon it was coursing through my body. I almost didn't know how I would continue to fight the urge until a knock on the door dragged me away from my thoughts. "That would be the Chinese," I said, while I supported her as she sat up so I could stand.

In a matter of seconds, I had paid and brought the bag of food in, setting it on the table in front of the couch, the scent of egg rolls filling the air. I grabbed some plates from a box that sat against the wall along with spoons and forks, and in a matter of minutes, the food was on the plates and we sat together, side by side, eating dinner.

We were halfway through dinner when Jessica placed her plate down on the table and wrapped her arms around herself.

"What is it?" I questioned.

"I feel so guilty, Ben."

"Why?"

"Well, if I hadn't run away, he wouldn't have come looking for me, and..."

"Don't say it, Jess. Don't you dare say this is your fault."

"How else am I supposed to feel? He is dead because of me."

"No way. He is dead because when he realized he had lost control of you, he lost control of himself. He was the one who ran in front of that vehicle, frantic because you had taken a stand. You didn't push him."

"I know."

"You're safe now, Jess. You can quit running. You can take your time, get back on your feet and start over. You can make your life exactly how you want it. You can take your time with the rest of this renovation even. There is no need to rush anymore. You can settle some roots here for a bit, if you want."

"I like that idea."

She sat back on the couch, curling herself up and closing her eyes. I couldn't help but stare at her. She was so beautiful, always had been, but she was very much off-limits to me, and I needed to remember that.

I got up and grabbed the plates, stacking them quietly so I didn't disturb her. Once that was done, I cleaned up and put the rest of the food in the fridge. When I turned around, Jess sat on the couch quietly staring at me. I smiled at her, waiting for her to smile back, but she just watched me.

"I guess I should get going. It's getting late," I said, shutting the lights off over the counter. The only light now was from the TV.

"Please stay."

"Oh, Jess, I don't think that's a good idea with everything that's gone on today. I think it would be best for you to get a good night's rest. Besides, I have an early morning, and most of my appointments are across town."

"I don't want to be alone tonight." Her eyes begged me and wore me down within seconds. "Please, Ben," she said, grabbing one of the blankets that lay on the back of the couch and covering herself with it.

Her soft, sexy begging voice sealed the deal. I walked over to her and smiled down at her, smoothing her hair off her face. "Okay, I guess I can stay for a bit."

I lay down on the opposite end of the couch, one hand behind my head, the other resting lightly across my abs, as I relaxed into the soft couch. I reached and pulled the spare blanket off the back of the couch above me and sprawled it over me.

We lay in quiet watching TV for a bit, and then Jess got up. She gathered her blanket in her arms, and without a word, she slid in beside me, rested her head on my chest, and curled up under the blanket.

I couldn't help myself. Lying there with her beside me, I wrapped my arms around her. I didn't fight it. She stared up at me, her hand resting on my chest, and I leaned in and gently grazed her lips with mine. Her body responded in a way it hadn't the other night by pressing into me. My hand resting on her cheek, I kissed her a little deeper than before, my tongue parting her lips, washing through her mouth, she let out a little whimper, which went straight to my cock.

Chapter Sixteen

It had been two weeks since the accident that had killed Kendrick, and I had found an unfamiliar sense of freedom. I had told Ben that the renovation didn't need to move as fast now, so his crew could take their time. Even though I knew I couldn't stay here forever, I wanted to enjoy Ben's company for as long as time would allow.

Over the last couple of weeks, we'd had dinner together almost every night. After dinner he would stay and watch movies with me late into the evening. Other nights we'd spend the evening curled up together on the couch talking.

I yawned as I pulled my hair up into a ponytail and slipped into my favorite pair of jeans. Ben had left late last night, and I had to be up early this morning to make sure the place was ready for the guys. I glanced at my reflection in the mirror and smiled. For the first time since I could remember, I was finally feeling a little like the person I used to be.

I carried my empty coffee cup into the kitchen, passing by the box of donuts and other sweets I had picked up at Mad House Coffee early this morning for the crew. I reached into the box, grabbed a cinnamon roll, and took a bite of the gooey treat. Since Kendrick was gone and Ben had been around more, I didn't feel as guilty eating things like this because he never made the comments Kendrick used to. Instead, he encouraged me to eat them. I had just filled my coffee mug and sat down with my gooey treat when I heard Ben's voice along with the rest of the crew enter.

"Morning?" he called, as he stepped around the corner.

"Oh, good morning." I smiled as he set his tools down on the floor. I couldn't help but check him out as the guys followed in behind, smirking. They were putting the finishing touches on the bathrooms today and then would start on the kitchen.

"I got you guys some donuts this morning, and as always, there is coffee."

"That is great! Thanks." Each of his guys grabbed

a donut from the box and some coffee and went straight to work, leaving Ben and me alone.

Ben smiled at me and walked over, leaning in for a kiss. "Hm, you taste good," he muttered, going in for another. "Kinda like cinnamon and sugar."

I giggled. "You caught me," I said, smiling up at him. "They are so good."

"Yes, that they are." Ben wandered over to the kitchen and poured himself a cup of coffee. I watched as his muscular arm flexed as he tipped the coffee pot. He winked at me and then heard a crash in the bathroom followed by a string of curses.

"That doesn't sound good." I giggled.

"I better go see what they broke." He placed his mug down on the counter and went running to see what the guys had done.

I laughed to myself as I watched him dart off while I opened the book I had been reading. I had just gotten into the book when the phone rang, causing me to jump. Reaching for it, I checked the display saw that it was Malone Law. I was still dealing with much of my grandfather's stuff, but after Kendrick had died, I had asked Hunter to look into things with Kendrick's lawyer.

"Hello," I answered.

"Jessica, it's Hunter Malone. How are you doing?"

"Hi, Hunter, I'm good, thanks. Yourself?"

"Good thanks. So I have some news for you. I finally got in touch with Kendrick's lawyer. We had a long talk, and he finally got back to me with some answers. So, apparently, Kendrick had a will. The excellent news is that you're named sole beneficiary, so everything is yours. Granted, that no one contests it. However, there is one caveat. You need to go back to LA to sign everything."

I couldn't believe my ears. Everything was mine? The condo, the furniture, the money, everything!

"Any idea on the worth?" I questioned.

"Over twenty million, taking into account the business and properties."

I just about choked. Really, it shouldn't have been an enormous surprise, but it was. Kendrick had never told me about the business. Honestly, he had never told me anything. I'd never seen bank accounts, or business statements. He had simply popped me onto my weekly allowance and led me to believe that things were tight. "When would I need to do that?"

"Honestly, the sooner the better. The quicker it's done, the less chance that someone will come out of the woodwork trying to claim things."

"Is this something that I can do on my own, or do I need you to be there."

"Well, if it is something you are comfortable doing on your own, go. However, if you feel that this lawyer isn't too honest and you want representation, then I'd have no problem meeting you there."

"Do I need to decide right now?"

"Like I said, the sooner the better, honestly. He wanted me to call him back after speaking with you to confirm a date. My schedule as well is getting a little hectic."

I looked around at all that still needed to be completed on this place and bit my lower lip. I could always just give Ben a key, I thought to myself. I trusted him to get everything done. "I guess I could meet with him next week. Perhaps on Tuesday."

I glanced at the calendar. I would need to arrange a flight as soon as possible, I thought to myself.

"Did you want me to meet you there? I can clear my Monday and Tuesday."

"Might be best. I know how corrupt Kendrick could be, so I'm assuming his lawyer will be the same way," I uttered. I wasn't lying. I knew Kendrick and the games he could play. For all I knew, he could have slipped in a document that gave up everything just as easily as owning everything. I knew nothing about legal terms.

"All right, Tuesday. I will fly out Monday night and meet you at his office Tuesday morning."

Hunter went over a little more information with me and gave me the address of the lawyer's office before I hung up the phone. I took a look around the apartment, and then I started searching or a flight back to LA for Monday night.

The following Tuesday, I met the very handsome Hunter Malone for the first time outside of Kendrick's lawyer's office in Malibu. We had an extensive meeting, and Hunter sat beside me explaining things as we went. We broke for lunch around one, and while I sat there eating a salad with grilled salmon, Hunter took his time going over all the legal documents. Once he was satisfied that nothing was amiss, he had me sign everything.

"Did you want to know what you just signed for?" he asked, gathering up the documents.

I nodded as I sipped some water.

"Well, you know about the business."

"Yes, and I don't want to own it, so..."

Hunter held his hands out to stop me. "No worries. We can dissolve it. I figured that might be easiest for you anyway and planned to talk to you about that once we had returned."

I nodded, smiling. "Thank you."

"Okay, so the business, all bank accounts. The good news is that Kendrick had zero debts, so aside from a three thousand dollar balance on a credit card, there is nothing else to pay off. There is also the condo in Beverly Hills."

"Yes, that was our home. All of that leads to twenty million?" I questioned.

"Not exactly. There is also the house out in Malibu Beach."

I frowned. I had no idea what Hunter was talking about.

"You look confused."

"I am. I knew about the condo, obviously, and the business, but I didn't know a thing about a place out in Malibu."

"Give me a minute." I watched as Hunter shuffled through the paperwork, coming to the part about the house, and spun it around to me. "He has owned it for almost eight years. You know nothing about it?"

I shook my head. Deep down, I now knew that my suspicions had been correct. He had probably been using that place as the location to meet up with other women. I suddenly wondered how often he had spent time there and how often he had lied to me about where he was off to.

"It's okay. Perhaps he mentioned it and I've just forgotten," I lied.

Hunter looked at me and then down to the paperwork in front of him. "You don't have to keep any of the properties. You can sell them if you wish or keep them and get rid of them in time. Whatever you do, I will be glad to help you along the way. When you are ready to tell me what's on your mind, just let me know."

After lunch, we had returned to Kendrick's lawyer's office and returned the paperwork. Then Hunter and I shared a cab back to the airport, and before we parted ways for our respective flights, he assured me that everything would be taken care of quickly and legally.

Once I was at my gate, I pulled out all of the documentation from the lawyer and sifted through it until I came to the address in Malibu beach. I glanced at my watch as an idea popped into my head. I shoved all my papers back into my bag and approached the boarding agent.

"I need to get on a later flight. Something has come up."

She smiled and took my pass and got on the radio.

Chapter Seventeen

Ben

I picked Jess up on Sunday night and headed to The Dive Bar for some drinks. One of the guys who was working on Jess's place was playing there with his band, like he did every Sunday night, so I thought it would be nice to support him. Plus, Jess was stressed, and I figured this might be a good way to help her unwind.

Jess covered her mouth, trying to hide a yawn, just as the music ended. I glanced at my watch, noticing that it was almost midnight. The next song started up again. While the music raged on, I got up and placed my hands on her shoulders. "Let's get going," I said, my lips grazing her ear.

"Did you have a good time tonight?" I asked,

opening the truck door. Jess had only been back a few days, but she seemed like she had changed after her meeting in LA. She seemed more relaxed, more carefree.

"I did. It was a lot of fun," Jess said, pulling her seatbelt across her chest. "The drinks were wonderful too." She giggled as I shut the door.

A loud clap of thunder and a strike of lightning flew across the sky as I ran around and climbed into the driver's side. "Looks like a storm is coming in."

Jess sat forward and looked up at the angry night sky. A flash of lightning lit up the black clouds. "Yeah, by the looks of things, it's going to be a bad one." She shrugged as a loud clap of thunder and another streak of lightning flashed across the sky.

I started the engine and pulled away from the curb, heading in her building's direction. We drove through the city, and just as we pulled up in front of the building, the skies opened and rain poured down. I parked as close as I could to the front doors, and then together, sheltered under my coat, we ran to the building and into the lobby.

I'd just pressed the button for the elevator when Jess turned and looked at me. She let out a contented sigh as we rode the elevator to the twenty-fifth floor. The doors opened, and we both stepped out, the doors of the elevator quickly closing behind us. The building shook from the loud clap of thunder, and then the hallway fell into complete darkness for a split second, until the emergency lights came on. I immediately sensed Jess's tension and put my hand on her back to let her know I was there.

"God, that was close," I mumbled.

"What was?" she asked.

"Can you imagine being trapped in that elevator?" I gave a nervous laugh. I'd always been claustrophobic, and just the thought of being stuck in that small space had me wondering if I shouldn't take the stairs back down when I left.

Jess looked at me and leaned into my shoulder. I placed my hand on her lower back, guiding her to her door. She searched through her purse, finally pulling out her key, and with shaking hands slid the key in the lock, opening the door. By the time we were inside, she was full-on shivering.

"Why don't I put the fireplace on and you get warm," I said, slipping off my shoes.

"What about you? You need to dry off too," she whispered, running her hands over my chest and tugging on the bottom of my wet T-shirt.

"Don't worry about me." I leaned in and kissed her forehead as if it were the most natural thing in the world for me to do. Only my lips lingered there longer than they should have. We'd kissed a couple of times over the last few weeks, but this one had been a slip. Kissing her forehead had been something I always used to do when kissing her good night before I left for home after a date. I slowly pulled away and watched as her tongue jutted out, wetting her lips.

Her eyes said it all, she wanted me, and in a matter of seconds, I feverishly attacked her mouth. Soon we stood wrapped in one another's arms. I pulled her against me as her fingers found their way into my hair. "God, you taste exactly how I remember," I moaned into her mouth.

Her hands gripped my hair and then ran down my chest, once again playing with the hem of my shirt, then I felt the tugging on my belt as she undid the buckle. She tugged until she had undone my belt and it came loose. I lifted her, allowing her to wrap her legs around my waist.

I wasted no time. I carried her down the hall to her bedroom. The second I put her down, she ripped my T-shirt up, pulling it over my head. I did the same to her. I could already see the outline of her hardened nipples through the fabric of her bra. I bent down as she walked backward toward the bed, and bit her nipple through her bra, and she inhaled sharply and dug her nails into my back. I quickly moved to the other one, repeating the action.

She fell onto the bed, sitting down. I could see the

desire in her eyes as she reached for me, grabbing my hips and pulling me between her legs. She looked up at me from where she sat, a playful glint in her eyes. Her fingers traced the waist of my jeans, finally falling on the button. She pulled it open, lowering the zipper, and ran her thumb over my already hard, aching cock. She continued stroking the tip with her thumb, then reached into my boxers, pulling my cock out. She held me in her hand for a moment and then wrapped her lips around me. I sucked in a breath and tipped my head back, biting my lower lip as she took me all the way to the back of her throat.

I glanced down and watched as her tongue ran along the ridge of my cock. She looked up at me as her mouth enveloped my cock for the second time. I felt like my heart would explode as I watched her close her eyes and continue sucking my cock.

I could feel my orgasm starting to build, and this time when she pulled me from her mouth, I pushed her back onto the bed. I grabbed her by the waist of the jeans and pulled her down to the edge of the bed.

In seconds, I'd ripped her jeans from her body and spread her legs, opening her wide. I dropped to my knees and licked up through her center, sucking that small bundle of nerves into my mouth. She sucked in a huge breath and let out a loud moan, gripping the blankets on the bed.

I kissed the insides of her thighs as her fingers ran through my hair. Sitting back on my heels, I dug my wallet out of my back pocket, ripping a condom from inside. I quickly tore the package open and rolled the condom down my cock. I couldn't wait to feel what it was like to be inside of her again.

My cock aching, I kissed the inside of her thigh again, moving up her body. I kissed her belly, quickly moving up and sucking one nipple then the other into my mouth before meeting her mouth. I made my way back down and knelt between her legs, gripped her hip with my hand, and ran my cock through her center.

"I want you, Ben. Take me."

"Fuck." The sound of her voice begging for me to take her sent shock waves through my body.

I placed myself at her opening and slowly eased into her. I wanted her to feel every single solid inch of me. She let out a slight whimper as I moved inside of her. I eased up and went slowly, interlocking her fingers with mine. I sunk deep inside of her and wrapped my free arm around her and kissed her neck. I felt her fingers dig into my back as I pumped slowly inside of her.

I could feel her tightening around me, so again I slowed my pace. I didn't want this to end already, even though I knew if she moved the right way I would explode. The deeper I went, the slower I moved, and the tighter she became. Soft whimpers in my ear, her nails digging into my back would be my undoing. I met her lips and silenced her moans as she came, tightening and spasming around my cock. My orgasm ripped through my body as I emptied inside of her.

When I finally caught my breath, I raised myself off her and met her lips, kissing her deeply. "I'll be right back," I whispered and pulled myself out of her.

A few minutes later, I returned to find Jess already curled up under the blankets, her eyes closed, as the storm still raged on outside. I climbed into bed behind her, pulled her into me, and wrapped myself around her.

Chapter Eighteen

I lay in bed watching the sunrise and thinking about last night. I could still feel his rough hands on my soft skin. I could still feel his arms around me, making me feel like I was the only woman in the world. I glanced over to see Ben sound asleep, snoring lightly beside me. He was lying on his stomach, his one arm hanging off the bed. I glanced at the clock. It was only four, but I had a bunch of things I wanted to get done today.

I got up, tiptoeing around the bed, careful not to wake him, making my way to the bathroom. I picked up our clothing that lay scattered in a path around the bed. I picked up Ben's shirt, tossing it to the chair that sat in the corner, then I grabbed his jeans. I folded them in half and felt something hit my foot. I looked down and caught a glimpse of something that appeared to be rolling and darted to grab it. Only whatever it was didn't roll. Instead it hung there, tied to a string, attached to the inside of his jeans pocket.

Flipping the jeans around, I grabbed the string and pulled the item up for closer inspection. There on the end was a ring, only not just any ring. It was the promise ring that Ben had given me when we were younger.

My stomach flipped as I stared at the ring that sat in the palm of my hand, memories flooding back to me. I dropped down to my knees, unpinning the object from the jeans, still studying it. I couldn't believe that he still had the ring. Had he had been carrying this ring around with him all these years? I glanced over to Ben and back to the ring in my hand and almost instantly I felt my stomach start to roll. Did he still love me?

"What are you sitting like that for? Did you lose something?" a deep, groggy, sleep-filled voice asked.

I could barely tear my eyes away from the ring I held in my hand, but when I eventually did, I was faced with Ben. A boy I had once loved who now had turned into a man. An absolutely gorgeous man in every way, one that was too good for me, one that I couldn't have.

The second our eyes met, I could tell from the look in his eyes, almost instantly, that he still had feelings for me. I doubted that they had ever left. How had I not seen it before now.

"What is this?"

"What?" he asked, rolling over onto his back and placing his hands behind his head.

"This?" I demanded, holding the ring between my fingers and shoving it into his face.

He swallowed hard, a hesitant look all over his face. Our eyes met, and I knew I was never supposed to have found it. He swallowed hard, his face going red. "Where did you find that?"

"Where did I find it? Are you serious? It was tied to a string, pinned into your pants pocket!" I bit out. "Were you planning on getting down on one knee this morning? Planning to confess your love for me?"

"Jess, calm down," Ben said, throwing the covers off his naked body and reaching for his jeans that lay on the floor where I'd left them.

"Don't tell me to calm down, Ben. What the hell are you still doing with this? You think things have changed suddenly? That I am going to run back to you with open arms?"

"I don't think that at all," he said, looking around the room for his shirt.

"Then why do you still have it?"

He stood staring at me, looking from me to the ring and back again. It was almost as if the words were caught in his throat. He wanted me back, and he had taken this opportunity, a moment of weakness, to sneak in and prey upon me. A moment where my life had been turned upside down to take advantage.

"Jess, I...."

I glanced at him. I could see the struggle in his mind and on his lips.

"Look, nothing has changed. I have plans, Ben, and they don't include running off into the sunset with you. It doesn't involve me staying here with you."

"Jess, that wasn't my intention. What happened—"

I held out my hand. I didn't want to hear any more of his excuses. "I do have a life, Ben. I have plans. My friend, Kate, has a job lined up for me once I return to LA. So, as soon as this project is finished, this place will be on the market and I will be gone."

"So once again, you are going to run, just like last time."

"This isn't like the last time."

"Sure it is. Look what happened all those years ago —a stupid idea of a wild promise and you took off. You are making the same mistake all over again. Just like last time, you are still the one dying to leave."

"Did you think because Kendrick is gone I would stay? My life isn't here. My life is back in LA."

"I never said that. Besides, you were the one who wanted the renovation to slow down. Last I checked you certainly haven't complained about being by my side for the last couple of weeks, or spending the evenings curled in my arms while we watch movies."

I stepped away just as he went to reach for me and held my hand up to him, stopping him. I turned away from Ben and looked out over the city as he continued rambling. He could say what he wanted. This was nothing like the last time. I could feel the anger building in me and blurted the only thing I could think of to say. "Last night was a mistake."

I regretted the words the second they fell from my lips. I couldn't even turn around to look at him, but I knew he was still there, and I knew I'd hurt him. I could sense his presence. I felt the tears burn in my eyes as I looked down to the ring.

"Wow. Really, Jess? Is that how you feel? That last night was a mistake? Your words, the way your body responded to me..."

I nodded. "It was a mistake." I knew the second I spoke my voice had betrayed me.

"Funny, I don't think this was a mistake. It was fate, Jess. Fate brought you back here, and fate made you call Sunset Builders. This is meant to be."

I squeezed the ring in the palm of my hand and ground my teeth together. "Get out!"

"You—"

"Just go, get out!" I said, turning around and meeting his eyes. "Here." I held out my hand that held the ring. "And take this with you."

He stood there looking at me and then ripped the ring from my fingers, grabbed his shirt, and headed out of the bedroom. I sat down on the edge of the bed. The sense of loss I felt only propelled the tears to start faster. The instant I heard the door slam shut, the floodgates opened. The life I'd known with Kendrick was gone, Kendrick was dead, he had a whole other life that he had kept secret from me. The life I'd once wished I could have back had been so close. I had just slept with Ben and I'd loved every minute of it. I didn't want to go back to the life I'd had in LA. I didn't know what I wanted, and to say I was beyond confused and extremely hurt was an understatement. Ben had no clue what he was getting himself into with wanting me back.

I looked around the empty apartment. I didn't want to be alone. I needed Kate, and I immediately picked up the phone and dialed her number.

I had explained nothing regarding Ben over the phone to Kate. All I had said was that I needed some company. Now, two hours later, Kate and I sat in the living room, each of us holding a hot mug of coffee in our hands. She'd been here half an hour, and all we had talked about was the opportunity she had for me when I returned to LA.

"All right, tell me everything. You called me over here, so spill it," Kate said, smiling.

The sunlight poured through the gigantic windows, warming us. "What do you want to know?"

"First, how did it go in LA?"

Sure, she had to start with that can of worms. "Well, everything is mine."

"Well, that is a good thing. So you have a home to go back to."

"I do, but I'm not sure I want to return to that condo. I think maybe I will get my own."

"Whatever makes you more comfortable, but it would be easier to just stay there." Kate took a sip of her coffee and looked at me over the rim of her cup. "You know, the pain of packing it all up. I hate moving."

"I know, so do I, and I don't look forward to that. I also found out that my suspicions were correct," I bit out.

"About?"

"Kendrick and his secret life. Did you know that he had a second residence? One that I didn't even know about over in Malibu Beach. I drove out to that residence after the meeting with the lawyer to look at it."

"What was the place like?"

I knew Kate had been dying to get a place out in that area. I was quiet for a moment, trying hard to decide how to tell her the news.

"Well, the house itself was gorgeous." I paused, determining that just blurting out what I had to tell her was for the best. "Before I came back, I got in touch with a listing agent and am listing both the house and the condo."

"I don't know what to say, Jess."

"How about those four little words that everyone dies to say when they were right: I told you so." I laughed to myself.

"Jess, I would never say that."

"Why not? It's the truth. You warned me years ago about Kendrick, and I should have listened." I shrugged.

We both sat there looking at one another until Kate averted her eyes.

"So, now that Kendrick is gone and you are now unbelievably wealthy, what are you going to do? Are you going to stay here?"

"No. Honestly, I don't know what I will do. I thought about going back to LA and grabbing a place out by the coast. Staying here really isn't an option."

"What? Why not? This is a beautiful place. That contractor is a cutie."

I blew out a breath. "Don't talk to me about Ben, Kate," I bit out.

"What? Why not? I am not saying anything that isn't true."

"He may be cute, but our history is just that."

"Did something happen between you two? You have been hanging out a lot."

I looked to Kate and shook my head. "Last night, things got a little out of hand. We slept together."

"So what? Did you have a good time?"

I could feel the blush rising over my cheeks. "I had a good time until this morning."

"Why, what happened this morning?"

"I found the ring he gave me when we were younger tied to a string inside of his pocket."

"So, let me get this straight. You inherit this place and end up hiring your ex to do renovations because you are planning to fix it up and sell it. The next thing you know, Kendrick is dead, and you inherit everything, want to sell the properties in LA, and dissolve his business. You end spending a shit ton of time with your ex afterward, accidentally or not fall into bed with him, and get pissed off when you find he still carries the ring in his pocket that he proposed to you with. Now you are going to leave because of that." Kate looked at me, one eyebrow raised.

"Oh, I'm not leaving here because of Ben, Kate." I took a sip of my coffee and set the mug on the table in front of us.

"Sure you are. I don't understand what you're so afraid of. I mean, the man is still carrying a ring he gave you years ago pinned inside of his pocket. I think it's sweet that he's still hung up on you. Obviously, he still cares for you," she said, taking the last mouthful of coffee.

I thought for a moment before answering her. The answer wasn't as simple as she thought. I was afraid of many things, so I came up with the cop-out answer. "It's crazy, Kate. He's been pining over me all these years. As for being afraid, I don't know the answer to that."

"Sure you do. Do you have feelings for him?"

"No," I quickly bit out.

Kate looked at me with disbelief in her eyes. "Either you're afraid to be with him or you're afraid of losing him. Which is it?"

"Kate, I didn't come here to find Ben. He never was and still isn't part of my plan."

"Let me ask you, when you moved to LA and met Kendrick, was marrying him ever part of your plan?"

"Goodness no."

"Exactly! So how is this any different?"

"Girl, did you not hear what I said. I have plans. Plans that I never accomplished because of Kendrick."

"Okay, well, you can say that, but I will tell you right now that the plans excuse is just that. Plans are meant to be broken."

"Not this time. This time I know what I want," I lied.

"So what are you going to do until they finish this place? I mean, from the looks of things, he still has a lot of work to do, which means he will be around."

"He does. Delaying him from finishing after Kendrick died probably wasn't one of the smartest moves."

"All right, so what is your grand plan to get you through this stage?"

"Ben has a key. He can let himself in and get things finished. I hoped that maybe I could stay with you."

"Jess, I'm not going to let you hide from this guy."

"Please, Kate, just this one favor."

Kate looked at me, exhausted from trying to argue. "Fine, but don't come down on me when you are sad and miserable after we return to LA."

Chapter Nineteen

Ben

I walked across the parking lot and climbed into my truck. I placed my hands on the wheel and rested my head on them, a mix of frustration, sadness, and anger building in me. Perhaps I could have handled the entire situation a little differently. I shouldn't have jumped to conclusions about her acting exactly like last time, except to me that was exactly what she was doing.

The longer I let the fact that I had just assumed things sink in, the more frustrated I became. I hadn't changed. I wanted what I wanted, and it didn't matter how she felt. I only saw what I wanted to see. I slammed my hands on the steering wheel, put the key in the ignition, and fired up the engine. I was halfway home when I turned my truck around. I needed to talk to my sister, and I needed to talk now. I glanced down at the clock. It was early for a Sunday morning, but I shrugged and hit the gas and sped toward her house.

"JULES! JULES!" I shouted as I banged on her front door. "OPEN UP!" I knew it was early, but normally my sister was up at the crack of dawn.

"COME ON, JULES, OPEN UP, PLEASE!" My shouting caught the attention of her neighbor, and she looked over my way and scowled, then picked up her morning paper, shook her head, and slammed her door shut.

"Where are you?" I muttered under my breath, raising my hand to bang again when the door was abruptly pulled open and I was faced with a sleepy-faced Jules.

"Ben? What do you want?" she huffed in her sleepy voice, tying her bathrobe tightly around her.

"I need to talk," I said, reaching for the screen door handle.

"Ben, did it ever occur to you that right now might be a terrible time, that I might have company?"

I thought for a moment. Jules wasn't seeing anyone, so the thought never crossed my mind. "No, it didn't, and honestly, I don't care. I need to talk."

Jules stood there looking at me and then finally opened the door and stood to the side to let me in.

"Come in," she huffed. "You probably woke the entire neighborhood up. You do know that I have a phone," she grumbled.

"I know, I'm sorry..." Suddenly, I felt bad for banging down her door.

"You look like you're going to cry. Come on, I'll put some coffee on."

I walked into her house and stomped across the kitchen with my boots on, getting ready to sit down.

"No, no, this isn't your bachelor pad. Boots off at the door," she chided, pointing to the front door as if I had lost my way.

I was about to get up and walk back to the door when she cleared her throat. I turned and looked at her and sat back down, taking my boots off, then got up and placed them by the front door.

"Fine, Mom, happy now?"

She nodded. "Broom is in the pantry. You can clean up the mud you tracked in here," she said as she dumped the coffee grounds into the French press.

"Seriously, Jules?"

"Yes, seriously, clean it up."

Finally, with all the mud swept up, I took a seat at her kitchen table and grabbed an apple from the fruit bowl and bit into it. She set a mug of coffee in front of me and sat down with her own across from me.

I looked at my sister and smiled. "I fucked up,

Jules." Not that it was funny, but if I didn't smile, I knew I would break down into tears.

"Something to do with Jess, I take it. What happened? Did you two have a falling out?"

I hadn't told my sister I had been spending time with Jess off the job. She hadn't known about the kiss —or kisses. She hadn't known about me spending evenings there before and after Kendrick had been killed. I'd kept it all under wraps for one reason, and that was the fact that she had warned me not to get involved. I knew she wouldn't approve.

"I slept with Jess."

Her eyes bugged out of her head. "You did what???" she shrieked, raising her voice to a pitch only dogs should be able to hear. "What part of don't push her did you not understand?"

"It wasn't like that."

"It sure sounds like it was like that. Jesus, Ben, you've been hired to do work in her apartment, not to sleep with her. What the fuck are you doing?"

I took a mouthful of the hot coffee, which burned on the way down, but I didn't care because somehow I figured I probably deserved it.

Jules sat there staring at me, waiting for a response, but before I could say anything, she cleared her throat. "Or have you been seeing her all along and just not telling me."

She hit that nail right on the head, I thought to myself. I ignored her and just began telling her my side. "We returned from watching the band last night and got caught in the storm. She was the one who had wanted to go to unwind, so I took her. Anyway, when I got her home, I walked her up to her apartment. I was planning to go home, but the power went out as soon as we exited the elevator. We went into her apartment and, sparing you the details, one thing led to another."

"Yes, please, please spare me the details," she said, running her hands over her face. "So what, you slept together. How did you fuck up?"

"Well, it wasn't something I did per se."

"Ben, what are you talking about?" Jules asked, getting rather irritated.

"She woke before me and found the ring I carry with me," I mumbled.

Jules closed her eyes as the words fell from my mouth and blew out a breath. "Oh, Ben."

The image of her sitting there staring down at the ring in her hand and her harsh words still ran wild through my mind. "She was so harsh."

"I can't say I blame her, Ben. Really I can't."

"What am I going to do. I want her back, Jules."

My sister looked up at me from her mug of coffee and shook her head. She was completely lost for words.

Monday morning, I arrived alone at Jess's apartment. I had wanted to smooth things over with her before the guys arrived. I knocked, but when no one answered, I used my key to enter. The apartment was quiet, and as I rounded the corner to the kitchen where I would normally find Jess, I found a note addressed to me on the counter instead.

Dear Ben,

I've gone to stay with my friend Kate until the renovation is complete. Please do whatever you can to have the apartment completed as soon as possible.

Jess.

I dropped the letter down on the counter and wasted no time calling Jules immediately. I had her send over a second crew, calling them off another job. We'd worked hard, putting in long hours to finish the rest of the job over the coming week.

Realizing she no longer wanted to see me, I didn't want to be there any longer than I had to be. Even though it hurt, I packed those emotions up and shoved them into the back of my mind and focused on the task at hand, as I had done once before because of her.

I'd put in late nights after the crew had left and worked until the wee hours of the morning of Thursday night just to get the job complete. Friday afternoon, the guys carried down the last of the tools and cleaning supplies, while I went through the apartment and checked over all the final touches. Once I was satisfied, I pulled out my phone and called Jules.

"Sunset Builders, Jules speaking."

"Hey, it's me. Jessica's place is finished. Can you please call her and have her stop by the office to sign off on everything?"

"Has she seen it? What did she say?"

I let out a breath. "No, Jules, she hasn't. At least not to my knowledge."

"Come on, Ben, you know the rules. The client has to be shown the finished product. It's your rule, not to mention you are the one who walks each client through their renovation."

I rolled my eyes at her brief lecture. She was

getting on my nerves and was on the path to being fired. I didn't care if that was my cardinal rule, a rule that my father had built his company on, which he had practically ingrained into me, but still, this job was different.

"Can you just do as I ask?" I barked.

"No, Ben, I can't. You are the owner. You are the one who sets the policies and procedures into place. You are also the one who adopted most of Dad's practices when we opened. Bottom line is she is still a client and still deserves the best we offer, regardless of any personal situation you may be in."

I squeezed my hand into a fist and clenched my teeth. "You know you always were a pain in my ass," I bit out.

"Yeah, well, pain in the ass or not, you know I am right. I will call her and let her know it's finished and that you will meet her there tomorrow to sign off on everything."

Chapter Twenty

JESSICA

I hadn't expected to hear from Sunset Builders so soon, but felt relieved to know that they finished the project. I glanced at my watch as I stepped into my apartment and set my bags down while I toed off my shoes. I was a little late and was surprised Ben wasn't already there. The message I had received from Julie had said that he would be here bright and early this morning. I glanced around, noticing that everything was back in place, and I was excited to see everything, but first, I picked up my bags and took them down to my bedroom, quickly emptying my clothes into the laundry hamper.

I'd had a chance while staying with Kate to look up a few realtors in the area, and I had found one that specialized in this building. She was supposed to be here this afternoon to take down all the details of the listing. She had asked that everything be tidy so she could also do some photos.

After quickly throwing in a load of laundry, I stepped into the washroom, taking a quick look at everything that had been completed, then I made my way into the kitchen. The last time I had been in the apartment, almost the entire kitchen had been removed. Now, one look at the brand new kitchen and it took my breath away.

I opened the cupboards to see that Ben had put away all the dishes that had been in boxes; everything including the food was organized neatly. Then I turned and looked at the colors we had chosen; everything complimented one another better than I thought they would, and as I looked around, a feeling of home surrounded me. It was the first time in years that I felt the meaning of the word.

I ran my hand over the smooth, cold marble countertops and smiled to myself. That was when I noticed a bouquet of red roses that sat in a vase on my counter. I was just about to look at the little card that was tucked inside the roses when a knock on the door pulled my attention away.

"Coming," I called as I made my way to the door,

opening it. Ben stood on the other side carrying a file in his hands. There was no smile, no words. He nodded and stepped inside, slipping his shoes off. I could sense the tension running off him and frowned as he made his way down to the first washroom. He stood outside the door and opened up the file he carried, turning to look at me. "Let's get to it, shall we? I have another appointment in thirty minutes," he said, looking at his watch.

He quickly rambled off a checklist of the items that had been completed in the spare washroom, checking each off as he pointed them out, and then made his way down to the en suite, doing the same thing. As soon as he had gone over everything in that room, he practically ran out of the bedroom to the kitchen, leaving me trailing behind.

I blew out a breath. His actions weren't helping anything at this point. I already he was upset over the entire situation, but acting like this was not helping anything. Instead of saying anything, I followed him out to the kitchen where he placed the file on the counter.

"All right, so, replacement of cupboards, backsplash, countertops, light fixtures, change to pot lights, and accent upper cabinets with lighting. Replacement of plumbing fixtures and flooring, paint. Everything looks good in here, right," he said, tapping his pen against the countertop, creating a sense of urgency for me to say yes.

I bit my lip. He had gone over it all so fast I had barely heard a word he said. "Yeah, I guess," I muttered.

"All right, then. Great, sign here then," he said, shoving the paperwork at me along with his pen.

I took the pen from his hand, checking to see if he looked at me, but he kept his eyes averted. I let out a breath and signed the contract in front of me and set the pen back down.

"Here you go," he said, sliding the bill in front of me. "All that leaves is the final twenty-five percent. A check or e-transfer will be fine."

I looked at Ben, who still refused to look my way, and walked over to my purse, pulling out my phone. I quickly entered the email address that was on the bill and sent the last payment through to him. "There you go. It's sent."

"Great." He reached into his pocket and pulled the key I had given him, setting it on the counter. "Well, I hope you enjoy the place for whatever little time you have left here."

Ben gathered the documents, picked up the folder, and walked to the door as quickly as he could. He slipped his shoes on and had one hand on the door handle, about to open it, when I touched his shoulder, stopping him.

"You did an amazing job, Ben. It will be hard for me to let go of something so beautiful."

"Yeah, I know all about it," he mumbled.

"How would you know?" I questioned.

"How would I know? Because I did it once," he said, finally turning and meeting my eyes. "It was the hardest thing I've ever had to do."

I knew he wasn't talking about anything material. He was talking about me, about us, and that comment combined with the hurt in his voice stung more than I expected.

"Ben... Can we..."

"No, I vowed I would never make the same mistake again, that I would never fall in love again, and I didn't. I was doing so well until you showed up here. Seeing you again made me realize that I have been in love with one woman my entire life. A woman who never did and never will love me back."

"Ben, please," I said, covering my mouth with my hand.

I met his eyes, those piercing eyes that I had never thought I would look into ever again. I didn't know what to say, all I knew was that I didn't want him to hate me.

"Please, Jessica, just let yourself fall in love with me. Don't make me lose you again."

"Ben, please, don't do this." I inhaled deeply. I could feel myself starting to shake. "The realtor is coming in an hour. I am supposed to pack up and get ready to move."

Ben looked at me and reached into his pocket and pulled out the ring, holding it up for me to see. "You asked me the other morning why I still carried this. I have carried this ring with me since the day you gave it back. I always just said it was a memento, but I've been wrong. It may not mean much to you, but for me it carried all of my hopes and dreams. It carries the ones I wanted to share with you. It carries every memory, every accomplishment, and every dream that's come true for me, except for one—you."

I felt the tears fall down my cheeks as I looked at him standing there holding this ring. I didn't want him to leave. I didn't want to let him walk away, but I still couldn't bring myself to say anything. I wiped the tears from my cheeks and composed myself.

"You know what else this represents?"

I couldn't respond because I knew if I did my voice would give me away and the tears would start flowing.

"It represents the promise of a new beginning. Our new beginning. I can build a business anywhere. It doesn't have to be here. It can be anywhere you want to go. What do you say?"

I shook my head and said nothing. I didn't have to. The knock on the door said everything. I knew on the other side of that door stood the realtor that was here to list the apartment. "I'm sorry, Ben. I have to deal with this," I bit out.

His gaze fell to the ground, and I knew in that instant I had broken his heart for good this time. He shoved the ring into his pocket, opened the door, and rushed off down the hall, almost knocking the lady to the ground.

"Jessica Hayward?" she asked, reaching out to shake my hand. "I am so excited to see this apartment."

I moved to the side for her to step in, but before I shut the door, I leaned out into the hall to see Ben standing waiting for the elevator. I heard the sounding bell that the elevator had arrived, and I watched as he turned to look at me one more time before he got in and left the building.

Chapter Twenty-One

Ben - One Month Later

I'd spent the next month working my ass off, trying to get all the projects done that we had fallen behind on. It was Friday afternoon, almost one month to the day that Jess had signed off on all the paperwork, and I was sitting in my office scrolling through the online paper, when an article caught my eye.

Jess had apparently gone back to LA. There was an image of her with her friend, Kate, raising two wine glasses and clinking them together. She looked happy. The article stated that they would star in a Broadway production of *Saltwater Moon*.

I'd gone home that night and gotten drunk alone,

passing out on my couch. It really wasn't that much different from every Friday night lately. When I woke, I got up and grabbed the laundry from the hamper and began sorting it, throwing shirts in the wash. Then I picked up my pair of jeans, the ring falling from the pocket. I took a minute to look at it, then I unpinned it from the inside of my jeans and set it on the table. I threw in the rest of the laundry, picked the ring up off the table, and took it to my bedroom where I put it in a safe place. In that moment, I'd decided I wasn't going to carry it around with me anymore.

I walked out into the living room and took a look around the place. Everywhere I looked was a disaster, and I decided in that moment that Jules was right; no woman would ever be interested in a guy who lived like this.

A knock on the door Sunday night surprised me as I dipped the mop into the bucket and rang it out. I turned to look over my shoulder to see Jules standing there.

"My God, you own a mop." She smiled. "Think I might faint."

"What's up?" I asked, ignoring her comment and sliding the mop back and forth across the floor.

She pulled the door open and stepped inside, keeping quiet as she stood and watched me.

"Something I can help you with?" I asked as I made my way closer to her.

"I tried to call you yesterday to see if you wanted to join Glenn and I at The Dive Bar, but you didn't answer. Everything okay?"

"Does it really matter?" I bit out, changing my direction so Jules could stand there a little longer and the rest of the floor could dry.

"Yes, Ben, it really matters."

I stopped what I was doing and rested my hands on top of the mop pole, keeping my eyes away from her. "I will be."

When I started mopping the floor again, I caught Jules staring at me through squinted eyes. "I'm not sure I believe you."

"Well, you should. I spoke to Glenn this morning. He's going to look after Sunset Builders for a month. I'm taking off, heading to the cottage. I need a break."

I'd expected Jules to fight me on this, but she nodded in understanding. "Good, I think a break will do you good. Glenn and I can get things taken care of. You have nothing to worry about."

I could sense the tension in the air between us as I finished the last few swipes of the mop across the kitchen floor. I did my best to ignore it, dumping the dirty water into the sink and filling the mop with fresh water and cleaner to wash the bathroom floor with. Jules still stood inside the door.

"What else did you want to say?" I questioned. I didn't want her staring at me with pity.

"About Jess..."

"Nothing needs to be said about Jess. It's over. You'll be glad to know that I've stopped carrying the ring too," I barked and picked up the bucket, carrying it into the bathroom.

"Ben."

"No. Listen, I should have known better. Instead, I let my weakness get the best of me. So, nothing needs to be said. She's gone back to LA, back to her life, and I have gone back to mine. It's enough about her. I'm going to take the month to heal myself, and now if you have something important to tell me, I'm all ears. Otherwise, this conversation is over."

Jules hung her head and nodded. "Guess I will see you in a month then."

I put the mop into the bucket of water and walked across my wet floor and pulled her in for a hug. "Thanks for being here. I don't say it often, but I love you."

"I love you too, Ben."

Chapter Twenty-Two

Jessica - Two Months Later

I SAT in my car on the side of the road staring up at the Welcome to Cottage Grove Lake sign. I hadn't seen that sign in years, and my stomach did an excited little flip. I wondered how much the small town I'd grown up in had changed. I wondered if it had changed as much as I had. I had driven out here shortly after I'd put both the condo in LA and the Malibu house up for sale. It had taken me almost the entire two months to get everything packed up and moved to storage so that I could have a saleable place. I'd hoped it wouldn't take me that long to go through everything that was in storage, but I was going easy on myself. It all didn't need to be done right away.

I took a sip of lemonade and was about ready to pull onto the road when my cell phone rang. I looked down at the display to see Malone Family Law was calling. I smiled to myself and answered, "Hello?"

"Jessica, good news. Both the sales of the Malibu property and the condo have been finalized," Hunter Malone's deep voice poured over the phone.

A funny feeling came over me. I wasn't exactly sure how I felt at the moment about the fact that the properties had sold. "Jessica are you there?"

"Yes, I'm sorry. I didn't expect them to move so fast."

"I'm just waiting on some paperwork to come through, but yes, they have sold."

"That's great. Did you need me to sign anything?"

"There will be paperwork, yes. I take it I can fax it over to your place in Vegas?"

"That will be fine. I'll be back next week."

"Okay, sounds good. Enjoy your time away."

"I will, thank you."

"You are welcome."

I hung up the phone and stared up once again at the sign in front of me. I could barely make out the sign, my vision was so blurry. Everything had changed in a matter of a few months. The entire life I'd known for the past few years had changed almost overnight. What I had wished for, I'd gotten.

I wiped my eyes, sucked in a deep breath, and eased out onto the road.

I turned down Pierce Avenue and drove slowly as I approached my old house. I slowed the car down and pulled over to the side of the road. The old white house had been painted recently. It was now a robin's egg blue color, and even though both my parents were gone, I still sat there expecting to see them walk out the front door.

I looked up to the window that used to be my bedroom, wondering if it still had the same flower-printed wallpaper I'd hung when I was in my early teens. I could almost hear the squeak in the floor that almost gave me away every time I snuck out in the night to go and see Ben. I smiled at the memory, then heard a bunch of voices. I looked in the rearview mirror to see a few kids on their way home from school.

I pulled away from the curb and continued on down through the downtown area. I passed the old ice cream parlor, the hardware store, the grocery store I'd used to work at, and then turned onto Mason Avenue.

I barely recognized the house Ben had grown up in. The entire front of the house had been redone. I looked down the driveway into the backyard. I did have the right house. There in the tree still sat the old tree house. I smiled to myself, thinking of the time I'd crept down his driveway after dark to the base of that tree, climbed up, and spent the majority of the night lying beside him, wrapped in his arms.

I cut the engine and climbed out of the car. It didn't appear anyone was home, so I slowly walked down the driveway. I got just past the house into the backyard when I heard a man clear his throat.

"Can I help you?"

I turned to see a man standing behind me. "Oh, hi. I'm sorry, I didn't know anyone was home."

"What can I do for you?"

"I'm sorry, I used to live in the area. This used to be a dear friend's house. I was just wondering if I could check out the treehouse."

"Oh, my dear, unfortunately, I can't let you climb up there. That old treehouse is unstable."

I looked up to it, a sadness creeping over me that I couldn't explain. Tears burned my eyes. "Thank you for your time. I'm sorry to have bothered you," I said as I turned, picked up my pace, and made my way back to my car.

I climbed in the front seat and looked once again down the driveway at the old treehouse, to the place where I'd lost my virginity. A tear crept down my cheek, and I started the engine and pulled away from the curb.

My chest ached as I continued through the streets of our old hometown. I drove past many business I remembered frequenting when I was younger, then some newer ones. Then I came across the Sunset Builders office. I smiled to myself, remembering how many times I'd sat out front waiting for Ben to return from his day with his dad. I didn't stop; I just kept driving, finally coming to the road that led out to that old cabin.

I slowed the car just as I passed the road. I tapped my thumb on the wheel, then I backed the car up and turned down the road. It was a longer drive than what I remembered. The road was still as undeveloped as it had been all those years ago. The longer I drove, the more the memories came flooding back, then the house came into view.

I slowed the car, seeing a for sale sign on the front lawn. The old cabin it had once been no longer looked the same. I put the car in park and cut the engine. I climbed out and stepped into the driveway, looking up at the house. I'd remembered seeing it when Ben and his father had started the remodel.

A breeze blew, and I could smell a mix of wildflowers and the lake. It transported me instantly to when Ben and I would sneak out here and lay under the stars.

I smiled to myself and toed my shoes off, stepping into the cool grass with my bare feet. It had been so long since I'd walked on grass. LA was nothing but concrete and so was Vegas. I stood and closed my eyes, listening to the sounds of nature and feeling the wind blow on my skin.

I sat down on the grass and lay back, looking up at the puffy clouds as they sailed by. I finally felt at peace, for the first time in my life. This was what I'd wanted— not LA, not Vegas, but this.

I'd lie in the grass for an hour before I felt a drop of rain hit my forehead. I got up and put my shoes back on then made my way to my car. I climbed in and looked up at the house, then over to the for sale sign. I pulled my phone from my purse and quickly dialed the number.

Chapter Twenty-Three

JESSICA - SIX MONTHS Later

I carried what would probably be the last two bags of groceries I'd need in Vegas. I placed them on the counter and quickly unpacked them, shoving everything into the fridge, and then I moved to the box I'd been packing. I'd finalized the sale of the cottage back in Cottage Grove Lake almost five months ago. The place had been neglected and needed some work, so I'd contracted Sunset Builders to oversee the work while I came back here to get the condo ready for sale.

I'd just finished packing the box and set it by the door for the movers to take down when the phone rang. I smiled when I saw John's number on the display.

"Hello," I sang into the phone.

"Jessica, I just wanted to tell you that all the renovations have been completed. The place is ready for you to move in when you're ready."

"That's great news, John." I smiled to myself, excited to get out of the city.

"I'll email you the final bill?"

"Yes, please. Oh and, John, you didn't say anything to Ben did you?"

"Not a word."

"Thank you."

We said our good-byes, and I looked around the condo. I was so happy with the decision I had made to sell those other properties and leave LA. However, I was much more excited to be returning to my hometown, where I felt very much at peace. I let out a breath as I looked around at all I still had left to pack. I grabbed the next box and moved over to the books that lined the wall and began boxing them up.

The next morning, I sat in Mad House Coffee, eating one of their cinnamon buns, while flipping through the paper. There on the fifth page was an article about Sunset Builders. I read through the article and flipped the page to see an image of Ben, looking prouder than he ever had, holding up an award he'd won. I smiled to myself as memories of him flashed through my mind. He had entered my mind a lot since

I had returned from Cottage Grove Lake. I realized that I missed him more than I had imagined I would.

That afternoon, I took a break from packing and drove out to Sunset Builders' main office. It had been months since I had spoken to Ben, or seen him for that matter. The last time was when he had stormed out of the condo, just as the realtor was coming to look at it. The pained look on his face was all I could remember.

Over the months that I'd returned, I remembered all the things that had made Ben so great, from his carefree, fun-loving attitude that he'd once had, to his loving and caring nature he still possessed. I thought about how it had felt to have been with him, how safe and complete he had made me feel. As I drove, a sense of calm came over me as I thought about the night we'd slept together. All those memories made me realize that he truly was the one. He held my heart, always had, and probably always would.

I pulled up to the Sunset Builders building and cut my engine. I climbed the stairs up to the main entrance and pulled the door open, stepping inside. The front desk was empty, as were the other offices, so while I waited, I looked around at the photographs on the wall. I looked at some houses that had been renovated back in our hometown, Ben and his father standing side by side looking so proud, then a picture of Ben and his dad in front of this location.

His father raising a glass to his son in a congratulatory pose.

"Oh geez, I didn't hear the buzzer. I'm sorry, can I help you with something?" I heard a voice behind me and turned to see Julie standing, holding a can of cola in her hand.

"Hi, Julie."

The look of shock on her face almost made me laugh.

"Jessica? What are you doing here? I thought—"

"You thought I moved back to LA, I know. I did, but things didn't work out the way I thought they would."

"Surprising," she scoffed.

"Is your brother here?"

A protective look came over her face as she stared back at me. "He's not, thank God. He doesn't want to see you, Jessica."

I nodded, the smile quickly fading off my lips. "I deserve that."

"Yes, you deserve that. The nerve of you, coming back here after you destroyed him, not once but twice," she said, putting the can of cola down rather forcefully and taking a step behind the counter. "Now that he has finally got his life together, you're here to do it all over again," she bit out.

"To be honest, Jules, I don't really think this is any of your business."

Julie let out a huffy laugh. "You don't? That's because you don't give a shit about him. Otherwise, you wouldn't be standing here in front of me right now. You'd accept the fact that he wishes to live his life in peace and happiness and you'd leave him alone."

A door slammed somewhere in the back of the building, catching both of our attention. The sound of footsteps and voices grew closer.

"Jules?" Ben called out. "Do you have the—" He stopped talking as he came around the corner and spotted me standing across from Julie.

"Jess? What are you doing here?" he mumbled.

I looked in his direction and then saw a woman following behind him. A funny feeling hit me in the pit of the stomach as I locked eyes with Ben and met hers. He had someone, he was finally over me, I thought to myself.

Ben turned to the woman who was behind him. "Polly, can you wait out in the car for a minute?"

She looked to me and then back to Ben and nodded her head before disappearing in the same direction they had come.

"Ben, just go with Polly. I'll bring you what you need in a minute. I have to take the trash out first," she bit out as she looked toward me.

Ben looked at his sister and then to me before turning to leave.

"Ben, I just want to talk to you. I didn't sell—" Ben turned to look at me, his eyes meeting mine. "I couldn't, not at first." I swallowed hard, a lump in my throat forming.

"What changed your mind?"

I smiled and ran my fingers through my long hair. "You."

Ben took a step toward me as his sister grabbed his arm. "Don't you dare. Just go outside. I'll take care of her," she bit out.

"Jules, this doesn't concern you." He shook out of her grasp and continued to make his way toward me.

Julie mumbled something under her breath and then left in a huff, leaving us standing in the front room. He stood in front of me, then he led me into what I guessed was his office where he shut the door, giving us some privacy.

The door clicked shut, and Ben turned to me, wrapping his arms around me. He hugged me tightly and then stepped away, looking at me. "So you kept the place, for what, a vacation home? What about the other properties?"

"Well, I moved back to LA for a while. Kate and I had gotten a part in—"

"*Saltwater Moon*. I saw the article," Ben said, leaning against his desk. "How did it go?"

"We'd begun practicing for the fall start, but something was missing. As the days passed, I realized it wasn't what I wanted. I thought it was, but everything about it felt so wrong. I still hadn't found a place to move into when the properties sold. I felt so lost, and the only thing on my mind was being here."

"I'm glad that you've gotten what you want and that you are enjoying it. Look, I have to get back to work. The guys are waiting for me out back. Was there something that you needed? Something that needs fixing at the apartment?" he questioned.

I shook my head. "No, Ben, it's all fine. I just came to tell you that I sold the place. I came to talk to you about what's missing."

"Missing? Now you wait a minute, before you start blaming my guys or me for taking something..."

I didn't know what to say, so I said the first thing that popped into my mind.

I shook my head. "That's not what I am here for, Ben. I'm here to tell you I found my missing piece."

"That's great, but..."

"I decided to go back home, to Cottage Grove Lake. I drove around the town, went and saw my house, yours... Did you know the old treehouse is still there."

Ben looked at me and shook his head. "No."

"It is, but I also went out to the old cottage. I took my shoes off, Ben, walked through the grass like I used to. Then I lay down in the front yard and looked up at the clouds. It was in those moments that I realized what was missing."

Ben looked at me like I'd lost my mind, waiting for me to continue.

"I bought the place. It was for sale. However, I can tell you just from being there those few minutes that you, Ben, are my missing piece."

"Jess, I—"

"Before you turn me away, let's just try us okay. No pressures, no expectations."

As I stood waiting for Ben to answer, I saw Jules glance our way. She scowled at me before sitting down behind her computer.

"Jess, it has taken me months to get over you."

"I know, and I know what I have I done, and I'm sorry for all the hurt I've caused you. Please, just let's try."

Ben stood there silent for a long time, and I sat there glued to him, waiting for what he was about to say. Then he looked at me and shook his head. "I'm sorry, Jess, but I'm seeing someone."

My heart sank at his words. It had taken me too long, and now I'd lost him. I fought back the tears that were burning my eyes, and I swallowed hard before nodding. "I'm happy for you..."

Ben looked at me, sadness in his eyes. He went to take a step forward to hug me, but I backed away. "I've got to..." I couldn't get the words out. I bolted from his office, running past Julie and out the front door. I ran down the steps and to my car, jumping into the driver's seat. In a matter of seconds, I'd reversed and was driving down the road away from Ben.

Chapter Twenty-Four

Ben

Some feelings never die, no matter how much you try to put them out of your mind. After Jess had visited me that afternoon, I'd went about my life, busy with business and dating Polly. She, of course, had all kinds of questions for me after Jess had left, and the more I tried to explain to her and assure her that everything was fine, the worse things got between us. Weeks had gone by, we grew distant, mainly because I hadn't been able to get the words Jess had said out of my head. Those words tormented me, finally driving a rift between Polly and me. Three months later, we broke up.

I returned to Cottage Grove Lake shortly after our breakup. I had set up a meeting with John to go over business, but that wasn't the only reason I had gone. Once again, I was looking for solitude. I'd been there two days when I'd decided to take a drive out to the old cottage. The sun was just setting, and I pulled my truck to a stop just before the driveway and looked at the little place.

I sat there for an hour staring at the soft light that poured from the windows. Then, finally, I climbed out of my truck and walked the rest of the way to the front door. I could see the TV on through the curtains and smiled to myself, then knocked on the door.

I waited, until finally, the door opened and Jess peeked out, a look of shock on her face as she stared back at me.

"Ben! What are you doing here?" she gasped.

I just stood there looking at her. She had died her hair dark brown, she had put on weight, and it was almost as if I'd been transported back through time. "You look good, Jess."

She opened the door a little farther, stepping to the side to let me in, shutting and locking the door behind me. We talked into the wee hours of the morning about everything that had happened. We talked about her marriage, what happened with the properties, and then I opened up to her about Polly, and how after she had visited me that things had changed. That I knew where my heart laid as well.

We rushed into nothing. We took our time getting to know one another again, becoming friends first, then we took things step by step as they came. Not rushing into things gave us the chance to learn things about one another that neither of us had known before, and gave us both a chance to accept them as they came. Our relationship, although intense at times, became one filled with patience, acceptance, and love.

It took Jules a long time to trust Jess, but she had promised me she would do her best to put aside all the ill feelings she held toward her. A year later, the two of them had become inseparable.

Jess began working at Sunset Builders in Cottage Grove Lake as the office manager, helping Jules with all the details to open our third location in LA. Glenn took over the Vegas location after proposing to Jules, John took over the new location out in LA, and I returned to Cottage Grove Lake.

I stirred the apple cider as it heated in the pot on the stove. Once it was steaming, I shut the burner off and poured the apple cider into the mugs that sat on the counter and set the pot back on the stove. Christmas music poured through the small cottage as the lights on the tree twinkled.

"Oh, you turned on the tree," Jess noticed as she

walked into the living room. She was wrapped snugly in her bathrobe as she curled up on the couch and flipped on the fireplace.

"Apple cider," I said, bringing over the mug. She reached up, taking it from me.

"Sounds great, thank you."

I sat down beside Jess and relaxed back into the couch, putting my feet up on the coffee table. I placed my arm on the back of the couch, and Jess set her mug on the table and quickly snuggled into me. It was a snowy night, and we sat there together, the only light coming from the Christmas tree, as we watched the snow fall outside.

I kissed her forehead as she rested her head on my shoulder. "Christmas Eve wouldn't be Christmas Eve without apple cider," she whispered.

Apple cider had been a tradition my mom had done for us kids before she had left. Every Christmas Eve she would make us each a mug, and we would sit and sip it while watching Christmas movies. "Why do you think I was late tonight?" I said, kissing her forehead again.

"I am glad you remembered," she said, sitting forward and grabbing her mug, taking a sip.

As Jess sat forward to put her mug back on the table, I reached into my shirt pocket and pulled the diamond ring I had purchased earlier this afternoon. I closed my hand around the ring as she sat back against me.

"What's in your hand?" she questioned.

I opened the palm of my hand and watched as her eyes went wide. "What do you say? Second time's a charm?"

She looked up at me and placed her hand on my cheek, kissing me. "Yes," she said, kissing me again before her fingers grazed the palm of my hand as she took the ring and slid it onto her ring finger.

Sitting forward, I set my mug on the table and then turned and picked her up. She let out a tiny squeal followed by a laugh as I carried her down the hall to the bedroom.

I was excited to start my life with her. Even though it had taken us ten years, we would finally be one. My hopes of riding off into the sunset with her had finally come true.

A Note from the Author

Dear Readers,

I'd like to thank you for taking the time to read Jess and Ben's story, Into the Sunset. I was listening to the radio one morning when they played Fallen Angel by Poison. The more I listened to the song, a clear vision of Jess popped into my head and that was how Into the Sunset was born. I am always fascinated with how my characters and stories come to me at times.

If you loved Into the Sunset, please take a quick moment and drop me a review. I always love to hear what my readers think.

Much Love,

S.L. Sterling

Coming Soon
Our Little Secret – June 20th
Our Little Surprise – August 15th

Both Books are currently available for preorder and a percentage of my preorder sales will be donated to charity for both books.

Preorder Here

About the Author

S.L. Sterling had been an avid reader since she was a child, often found getting lost in books. Today if she isn't writing or plotting, she can be found buried in a romance novel with a cup of coffee at her side. S.L. Sterling lives with her husband and dogs in Northern Ontario.

Want to keep up to date, join my newsletter.

For more information you can also visit my Website.

Join my Reader Group on Facebook
Sterlings Silver Sapphires

Other Titles by S.L. Sterling

It Was Always You

On A Silent Night

Bad Company

Back to You this Christmas

Fireside Love

Holiday Wishes

Saviour Boy

The Boy Under the Gazebo

The Greatest Gift

The Malone Brother Series

A Kiss Beneath the Stars

In Your Arms

His to Hold

Finding Forever with You

Vegas MMA

Dagger

Doctors of Eastport General

Doctor Desire

All I Want for Christmas (Contemporary Romance Holiday
Collection)

Constraint (KB Worlds: Everyday Heroes)

www.ingramcontent.com/pod-product-compliance
Lightning Source LLC
Chambersburg PA
CBHW030925210726
48290CB00007B/2080